PRAISE FOR HUNT FOR THE VIRGIN RAINBOW

'Feel the heat from the first page and instantly visualise the movie! You're in for the adventure of your lifetime. Mallory Cash is not your typical outback girl. She's a thief. Stealing the opal was easy, but the escape… K. M. Steele cleverly weaves a gripping adventure that will keep you turning the pages. Toss in a touch of romance, an interesting past and you've got all the ingredients for a bestseller. Keep them coming Ms Steele! We from the 'Sunburt Country' want more,' C. T. Mitchell, Author.

'A sprightly, engaging and highly enjoyable caper through the South Australian bush. We follow our (anti-) heroine, Mallory Cash, as she bears a precious and much-pursued opal and tries to juggle two very different types of dangerous men. This is a fun and atmospheric novel that holds the reader's attention and leaves them hungry for even more,' Prof. Nicholas Birns, Literature Faculty, New York University.

'A little lightness after a very heavy year. K. M. Steele has written an easy-to-read story that entertains with a novel tale of thieves chasing a precious jewel (and at times each other) across the wilds of Australia. Throw in a troubled female protagonist, a touch of romance, and a mysterious backstory and this book becomes a guaranteed crowd pleaser. The Hunt for the Virgin Rainbow is an all-rounder—it's accessible, enjoyable and, most importantly, doesn't take itself too seriously,' Candace Davis, Author.

Hunt for the Virgin Rainbow

K M STEELE

HAWKEYE

PUBLISHING

First published in Australia in 2021 by
Hawkeye Publishing.

Cover Design by Ellen Milligan.

Proudly printed in Australia by SOS.

ISBN 9780645084429

www.hawkeyepublishing.com.au
www.hawkeyebooks.com.au

1

MALLORY yawned and rolled her shoulders. The motorbike drifted toward the centre of the road. She corrected her line without urgency. The empty highway melted into the shimmering, heated nothingness ahead of her, Port Augusta no more than a distant memory. She squeezed her eyes shut against the glare, before surveying the unrelenting flatness on either side of the road. This last stretch to Coober Pedy was the most featureless, boring ride she'd ever taken in her life.

Four emus appeared on her left, running alongside the bike. Earlier experience had taught her to resist the urge to race them. Like the giant red kangaroos that covered jaw-dropping distances in one bound, these oversized birds had some speed. She dropped down a gear, waiting for the inevitable. There would be a point of no return when they darted across the road in front of her. Their long legs covered the ground in easy strides, making the feathery skirts on their rumps skip back and forth. One drew level with the bike, looking down its beak at her with an intense dinosaur eye. Her breath caught in her throat. The creatures in Australia were so alien. Some of them seemed frightening and impossible. All the same, the emus were a welcome relief from the monotony of the journey and would have continued to hold her attention if a dark lump on the side of the road had not appeared out of the haze.

As she came closer, the indistinct shape solidified into a dark green 4WD. Steam rose from the front of the vehicle and a tall well-built man stood at the back, his face barely visible behind fashion sunglasses and a white handkerchief tied around his nose and mouth. He waved frantically as she approached. She played it safe, moving toward the middle of the road as she slowed.

He ran toward her. 'The motor's blown. Can you give me a lift to Coober Pedy?'

The sound of his familiar voice sent an unpleasant jolt through her body. 'Derek? What the hell are you doing here?'

He pulled off his sunglasses. 'Mallory Cash? What are you doing in Australia?'

She gunned the bike. 'I asked first.'

'Oh, come on honey, this is hardly the time to play games.'

'I'm not playing. Remember what you did last time we had the pleasure of each other's company?' She rolled the bike forward.

He held up a pleading hand and stepped closer. 'Now come on sweetheart, that was over twelve months ago. Surely you're not still angry.' He took another tentative step. 'Come on Mal babe, for old time's sake?'

She hesitated. 'What are you doing here?'

'I'm on holiday of course. Who can resist the sights

2

and sounds of Australia?' He spread a hand toward the emptiness beyond the road.

She burst into laughter. 'Try again, buddy.'

He moved a step closer. 'Well if you must know, I've been looking for you, babe. I mean, really and truly searching. When I discovered you were heading down under,' he looked at her with melting eyes, 'Well, let's just say, I can hardly believe I've found you again.'

He took another step toward her. 'You've always been a hard one to pin down, Mal.'

She knew he was lying. His ability to manage it so well, and with such speed, could still stun her.

She shook her head. 'See ya, big boy. It's your turn to walk.'

She took off before he could keep working on her. He had his ways, did Derek. He would smile that beautiful 'trust-me' smile, and pin her to the ground with those dancing blue eyes. She would be putty, would end up giving him whatever he wanted. Well, not this time. She looked in the rearview mirror, saw him jumping up and down on the road, shaking a fist in her direction. She grinned and blew him a kiss. He'd be okay. Guys like him always fell on their feet.

Long after she left Derek behind, his presence in the middle of Australia continued to bother her. He wasn't the kind of guy who liked to holiday in out of the way places. Hanging with the rich and famous, being seen with beautiful women in Cannes, that was more his style. Was he working for someone? Was he following her?

She pushed the last idea away. Ridiculous to think Derek had any interest in her. Their moment was well and truly gone. He made it abundantly clear the last time they were together that they would never be an item again. Professional reasons though, now that was another matter.

The facts clicked over in her mind, settling on a disturbing outcome. It was impossible to know who had employed him, or how he came to be where he was, but there was no doubting he was here for the same reason that had drawn her to Australia. He was hunting the Virgin Rainbow.

Mallory accelerated, leaving the discomfort of discovering Derek behind as she sped into the desert. The pale mullock heaps near the outskirts of Coober Pedy appeared out of the haze and she slowed to look. She'd done her homework. The mullock heaps meant she was getting closer to her goal. She pulled the bike over, taking a moment to stretch her legs, and wonder why some of the world's most beautiful gems came out of a landscape with indescribable animals, enormous tracts of nothing, and garbage dumps. She cast an eye over the flat, empty land beyond and decided that the mullock heaps might come in handy in the future. They continued as far as the eye could see, hiding any number of abandoned dreams and broken promises in the mine shafts dotted throughout the heaps. They were the perfect place to run in an emergency.

She walked back to her bike, baulking at the sound of an approaching vehicle. The stuttering engine was almost drowned out by loud music, whistling and raucous female laughter. She waited, watching the empty road with interest until an old school bus, complete with a pair of men's trousers on the antenna, appeared. Garish flowers and chickens dressed in red bikinis decorated the sides of the vehicle. As it drew closer, women appeared at the windows, their heads covered in gossamer veils. They waved and yelled at her in flat, indecipherable accents as the bus passed. She caught a glimpse of a man gyrating in the middle of the bus, his muscular torso covered in female hands. As the vehicle passed, a sign on the back proclaimed, *The Chick Coop entertaining hens from PA to Coober Pedy for 20 years!*

Her first Australian hen's party in action… From what Mallory could see, they were a little different to the bachelorette parties she'd attended in Canada. She chuckled. The poor guy on the bus would be more than earning his money to keep those ladies happy. She jumped on her bike and waved at the screeching women as she overtook them on the way into town.

***

Derek watched Mallory ride by and silently promised to make her pay. One of the hens jumped out of her seat and grabbed at his groin as he danced along the aisle between the seats. He slipped from her grip, waving a finger at her like a school headmaster. The bus hit a bump on the highway, throwing him off balance. He bounced into the woman and put his hands on her waist to steady her against the rocking of the bus.

She laughed and threw her arms around his neck. 'We got us a live one here, girls!'

He peeled her hands off his neck with difficulty and moved toward the driver. He was almost close enough to get her attention when a girl lying across one of the front seats put her long legs across the aisle. 'Not so fast, sailor. There's still a mile of fun before we reach Coober Pedy.'

He turned without argument and danced toward the

back of the bus. When it had first pulled over on the highway, he was certain the bus was the answer to his prayers. The women cheered as he climbed the steps and he thought he was more than set for an enjoyable journey. What more could a man ask for than a busload of women on the prowl? He expected light flirtation, a lot of attention, perhaps a phone number or two. But these women were like none he'd ever met. They'd taken his trousers hostage and told him to dance for his fare. The bride was already face-down on the back seat, her auburn hair tangled amongst her veil, her skirt up around her buttocks. Her loud snoring was a source of great enjoyment to her companions.

As the women uploaded photo after photo of the backseat sleeping beauty, and their captive "desert pirate", to the net, Derek thanked God they let him keep his bandana and sunglasses. The last thing he needed was someone recognising him. It was bad enough that Mallory had seen him.

He stepped around another amorous hen and wondered why Mallory Cash was in Australia. She loved wild, untouched places, so perhaps it was coincidental. Maybe she just wanted some time out to get over him and had chosen the back end of nowhere to do it.

No, even at his most egotistical, he knew she had moved on long ago. His gut told him something else was afoot. If she wanted time out, she'd go home to Canada, to those frozen mountains she loved so much. He felt sure she was here for the same reason as him – The Virgin Rainbow.

'The virgin whattie?' A tiny blonde swayed in front of him, her beer bottle tipping and dribbling down the front of her dress. 'Did you hear that girls? This fella wants a virgin!' She put a sympathetic hand on his shoulder. 'Jeez, sorry mate, you picked the wrong ride.'

The women erupted in laughter. Derek cursed his inability to stop muttering when he was angry. He grabbed the blonde, twirling her around and singing a pirate song until she giggled and shrieked. The flurry of photography and mirth that followed deflected attention from his slip of the tongue.

2

MALLORY rolled into the sleepy town that looked as overheated as it felt. There were few cars and even fewer pedestrians. The main thoroughfare was broad and straight with red dust meeting tarmac, and sidewalks flanked by low, utilitarian buildings. Occasional trees and hedges provided greenery, which stood out among the different shades of red and brown. Signs along the street offered opportunities to buy, view, mine and polish opals, visit opal museums, and take opal tours. She slowed at the Underground Art Gallery and carefully surveyed the area. The giant rainbow coloured boomerang and small bunker entrance didn't suggest the kind of place where a person would find much of worth, but she figured looks could be deceiving in a place like this.

Mallory parked the bike behind an old bus near the gallery entrance and went down the stairs, stopping short at the amazing space and coolness of the underground chamber. Despite the spaciousness, she felt her old enemy, claustrophobia, closing in and had to remind herself that she could leave whenever she wanted. She forced herself to focus on the fiery coloured gems on display. She had read all about Australian opals, but nothing prepared her for the light and colour of the real thing. Their warm blues, reds and yellows made her fingers itch. They came in a dizzying range of shapes, sizes, colours and shades, and seemed suited to everything from the simplest, to the most intricate setting. She wandered through the display, fascinated by the back story of the town and the gems so coveted by its occupants. She also took the time to do a thorough check for alarms, cameras and security guards as she went.

Before she left, she approached the guide at the counter. 'Is it true the famous Virgin Rainbow is coming back to Coober Pedy?'

The guide pulled a pamphlet from under the desk. 'Yeah, take a look at the dates and viewing times and stuff. We're real excited to have our rare opal back in town.' She tapped the pamphlet with the end of her nail. 'It glows in the dark, you know.'

Mallory widened her eyes. 'Really? I'll try to come back to see it for sure.'

The guide smiled. 'Yeah, I reckon you should.' She leant on the counter, settling in for a chat.

Mallory scooped up the pamphlet and moved away. 'Thanks for your help,' she said.

Once outside, she walked around the entrance. The job required plenty of thought. There was no way she was getting trapped underground. The idea of being under there with the doors locked was terrifying. Sure, there wasn't much security, but there was only one entrance, and it would have to be used for the job. She had no intention of digging her way in or blowing the place up.

Her tummy rumbled, making her glance at her watch. If she didn't hurry, she'd be late for the meeting. She jumped on her bike and after a final perusal of the carpark and surrounding buildings, cruised onto Hutchison Street toward the Desert Cave Hotel.

The room was booked, as Trafford had said it would

be, but he'd booked her into an underground suite. She insisted on moving to an aboveground room, despite the clerk's protests that she was missing the experience of a lifetime. People in her line of work didn't get a lifetime if they slept in places with no possibility of escape. She took the key and picked up her rucksack, eager to get to her room and wash the road dust off.

'Hey miss, I almost forgot. I have a letter for you,' the clerk called out.

Mallory grabbed the letter and pushed it into her rucksack. She was about to turn around when she caught sight of a slightly-built man with quick, silent movements and sharp features entering the foyer. He was only a centimetre or two taller than Mallory and luckily for her, had his eyes on his watch when she spotted him. She squatted down, keeping her back to him as she pushed her hand into her rucksack and pretended to search for something.

Jimmy the Cat came to the counter, stopping beside her. She stared at the sharp crease in his trousers. Good quality Italian cloth, the kind an undertaker would wear. Her hand started to shake inside the rucksack.

'Hey up guvner, I need to find the Opal Cave.'

No problem, sir. If you come to the door, I'll point it out to you.'

Jimmy turned around and almost fell over Mallory. 'Bloody hell! Get off the floor before you hurt a body.'

'Sorry,' she mumbled.

He remained motionless beside her. She kept her head down; saw her face reflected in the high polish of his shoes. She closed her fingers around the knife in her rucksack, hoping the sunglasses and blonde wig she wore were enough to ensure he didn't recognise her.

'Daft mare,' he grunted, before walking away.

She loosened her grip on the knife when he was out of sight. Jimmy wasn't interested in stealing jewels unless they fetched at least five million. All the same, he had to be in town for the Virgin Rainbow, which meant he was working for someone else: someone who had paid him a lot of money to deliver. She shuddered. The last time she saw Jimmy was five years ago in Paris, when he hit a jewellery store with a gang of mercenaries. The carnage was terrible. The gunfight had raged for hours. She was unfortunate enough to be undertaking a small job at another store on the Rue de la Paix and almost became collateral damage, just by being in the wrong place at the wrong time. The memory of him running along the street, shooting anyone that moved was etched into her mind. He had stopped momentarily in front of the jewellery store she was robbing, and stared right at her, smiling that shark smile as though they shared a private joke. She had the strangest feeling he recognised her, although she knew that to be impossible. All the same, she always erred on the side of caution. He must not see her.

When she reached her room, she opened the letter, read the instructions and cursed. The mystery of Derek's presence in the desert was explained. She thumped the bed and cursed again. If Trafford had informed her she would be working with Derek James, she would have said no to the job. Now it was too late to do anything about the situation. She grabbed her lighter, burnt the paper and flushed the ashes down the toilet. Then she jumped in the shower, scrubbing at her body and stewing on the turn of events.

Derek had been so close to her once, and they were a good team when it came to getting a job done, but that was history. There would be no more wild days and steamy nights together. No more long showers in the afternoon with Derek, followed by glorious games of hide and seek in the bedroom. No more romantic meals where the sexual tension would build until she thought she would explode. The memories brought every nerve-end alive. She turned the water to cold, letting it stream over her face until she calmed down. She turned the tap off, rubbing the towel

11

over her slim body with unnecessary vigour. The only thing she could do was go to the meeting tonight at the Opal Inn and hope that they could get the Virgin Rainbow, get to the rendezvous point, and go their separate ways as quickly as possible.

After her shower, she rummaged through the backpack, pulling out her emergency dress. She held the gossamer material against her body and imagined Derek taking it off her.

'No, no, no!' she muttered, shoving the dress into the bottom of the backpack. Instead, she chose a mousy wig of matronly grey curls, thick glasses, brown contact lenses to cover her distinctive violet eyes, and a shapeless, floral dress that added fifteen pounds to her frame. She checked her image in the mirror, and pulled her mouth down at the aged, unfit woman who stared back at her. She felt confident Jimmy the Cat, or even Derek for that matter, would not recognise her if they passed her on the street.

***

The bus ground to a halt in front of the Comfort Inn. The doors wheezed open and the driver, who appeared to be the same vintage as the vehicle, clambered down the steps. The driver peered up at the once white trousers, limp and coated with red dust, on the antenna on top of the bus. She frowned up and down the street, until she spotted a young boy leaning against a telephone pole.

'Hey you, young fella,' she called out. 'You want money?'

He nodded, laughing as he ran to the bus. She pointed to the antenna while he hopped from foot to foot on the burning tar.

'Climb up mate, and grab those trousers. There's a dollar in it.'

The boy climbed up the side of the open door and swung onto the roof. He grabbed the trousers, flicking them around his head with a whoop, before throwing them down. The bus driver reached into her baggy shorts and flicked him a dollar after he jumped down. He took off up the street without a backwards glance.

The interior of the bus was eerily quiet compared to earlier in the day. Derek sat on a seat near the front and kicked at the sea of cans and wrappers on the floor, while he surveyed the sleeping women surrounding him.

The bus driver climbed up the stairs, complaining about her knees and ankles as she moved. She beckoned Derek, tossing his trousers over the back of a seat. 'Here, pet. Get going before the ladies find their second wind.'

He grabbed his pants, pulling them on without comment.

She put a hand on his forearm. 'It wasn't all bad was it, pet? Better than dying alone in the desert, eh?' she smiled. The gap between her front teeth reminded him of his Aunt Florence, who had always given him chocolate and sips of beer when his mother wasn't looking.

He softened. 'Yeah, better than a slow death with the buzzards, I suppose.'

She roared with laughter. 'You'll do. You're all right for a Pommie, mate.'

Derek waited until the bus turned the corner before stepping away from the front of the Comfort Inn. It didn't take long to establish where he needed to go and he was relieved to discover he wouldn't need a car to get around Coober Pedy. When he reached the Mud Hut Motel, he conducted a full inspection of his room for cameras and bugs, before opening the letter given to him by the clerk. He laughed, the sound mirthless and sour in the cooling afternoon. Right now, his prospects weren't looking good. Working with Mallory was going to be worse than the bus trip to this Godforsaken place. Then again, he might be able to work the turn of events to his favour, have her eating out of his hand again.

He took his time showering, enjoying the peace of the

ritual after a day trapped on a bus with a pack of crazed, drunken women. Afterwards, he filled the sink and lathered his face, shaving with deliberate care. Then he searched the cupboards, smiling with glee when he discovered a hairdryer. He styled his hair for longer than any man should, but he had always believed in the importance of good grooming. He splashed on a liberal dose of aftershave, pulling a face in the mirror when the stinging liquid hit his skin, applied his signature cologne, pulled on a shirt so crisp it looked as though it had just been laundered, and flicked through the buttons with ease. Finally, he scowled at his footwear. Far from ideal, but he had no other option. He lifted each boot to the rim of the sink, brushing off the dust with a face washer, before straightening and practising his best smile in the mirror with a final, satisfied nod. It was time to play his ace. He'd broken Mallory's defences before. Tonight would be like taking candy from a baby.

***

Mallory watched Derek push through the door and swagger toward the bar. Every woman in the place turned, staring as he stood for a moment, fully aware of the feminine admiration he caused. Every hair on his blonde head was perfectly placed and his blue eyes radiated the kind of promise most women found irresistible. He looked like he had just stepped out of a magazine in jeans that displayed muscular thighs and a narrow waist, and a crisp white shirt that set off his tan to perfection. *God, he's a cocky son of a bitch. But smoking hot with it.* She pushed the last thought away. He leant his back against the bar and winked at a leggy redhead near the jukebox, before scanning the room while he waited for his drink. His gaze may have appeared casual to the uninitiated, but she knew he was methodically scrutinising every woman in the bar. Mallory concentrated on looking bland while his eyes passed over her without hesitation. He kept scanning, searching every female face, before turning toward the bar. The redhead sidled up to him, leant over and spoke in his ear. He replied, and she laughed as if she had just heard the joke of the year.

Mallory's moment of triumph was tinged with jealousy at the scene. God, he could still get to her, but if he didn't recognise her, nobody would. She relaxed, finishing her drink while the redhead flirted and gave him her number. After the woman left, she watched him check the mirror and tap the bar with his knuckles. One leg jumped rapidly, a nervous tic he hadn't quite mastered, while he watched the door. She thought about staying in the corner for a couple of hours watching him sweat, because whether he liked it or not, he couldn't ditch her this time. The letter had been clear. They wouldn't get paid if they didn't work together.

After fifteen minutes, she stood slowly, the way a woman who was older and heavier would. She walked to the bar, shoving into him as she ordered her drink. He shifted to give her more space, turning his back to indicate she need not bother apologising.

She tapped him on the shoulder. He turned a dismissive look on her.

Don't I know you?' she asked.

'No,' he said. He turned away then stopped, staring at her in disbelief. 'You're kidding, right?'

'Nope. You didn't even begin to see me, buddy.'

'Well, who would? You've put on weight. You look like a bag lady.'

'Ouch! Take it easy with the charm, already.'

He shook his head. 'Sorry, but when you look like that, you are quite safe with me.'

Disappointment coursed through her. She shook it off. He'd played her too many times. She should be happy that her current disguise as the blandest woman on earth was the perfect defence against his charm.

She tipped her head toward the table in the corner. 'Let's talk.'

Several women in the bar watched them walk toward their table. She could almost hear them thinking, *what has she got?* It would be funny if the situation was different, but right now Derek's insistence on looking good was a liability.

When they sat, she leant close and hissed, 'Do you have to draw so much attention to yourself?'

'You never used to complain.'

'I saw Jimmy the Cat in town today.'

'Shit!'

'I know. I can't think who he'd be working for. Any idea?'

Derek shook his head. 'He's a problem we didn't know we had. He could screw it for us.'

She raised her glass. 'First point of order agreed, so maybe you should tone down the bachelor of the year look, yes?'

'You've got your disguises, sweets. I have mine. Sometimes the best way to stay below the radar is live large.' He leered and wriggled his eyebrows at her.

'Seriously Derek, I don't know how you ever managed to avoid consequences.'

He laughed and put a hand on her leg. 'Come on Mal, I think you may have some idea.'

She coloured and shook him off. 'You are such a tart.'

His eyes sparkled with feigned innocence and his voice dropped a seductive notch. 'I play to my strengths, babe.' His smile widened. 'How about you?'

Her heart skipped a beat. 'Whatever. Let's get down to work.' She pushed her empty glass out of the way and folded her arms on the table. 'I did a recce on the gallery. It's a soft target except for the fact that it's underground.'

He frowned. 'Why didn't you wait for me?'

'I didn't know I had the pleasure of your company at that point in time.' She pulled the pamphlet out of a pocket in her voluminous dress and passed it to him. 'Take a look. It's arriving the day after tomorrow. They'll probably beef up the security. The biggest problem is the fact that there's only one way in, and out.'

He nodded. 'We'll have to hang low until Wednesday.'

'No shit, Sherlock. What did you have in mind?' Mallory didn't want to admit it, but she was entertaining the thought of taking Derek back to her room. Reliving the old times, when they meant something to each other. Pretending they still had something going on would sure beat hanging around in a hotel room alone, watching regional television and eating takeaway.

He inspected the map of the gallery she had drawn on the back of the pamphlet, completely unaware of her moment of weakness. She listened to his plan and knew the precise logic of his mind was ticking over each detail.

Her mind drifted back to the last time they'd seen each other. He'd left her on the side of the road in Cuba without a second thought for her welfare. He was the same old Derek: cold and logical when he was working, hot and erratic in his personal life. She wouldn't go down that path again, not even for short-term pleasure. The thing to do was stay focused, so they could nail this job and get far away from each other before anyone figured out what had happened.

***

The sound of metallic scratching outside the window woke Mallory. The darkened room was cloaked in an eerie stillness. She moved her hand under the pillow, closed her fingers around the Glock, and rolled onto the floor near the bed without making a sound. The scratching stopped. She breathed lightly in the silence, all senses alert. The scratching was replaced by a sharp tapping under the same window. She crawled across the room, pressing against the wall below the glass. A low sing-song voice started, barely audible above the tapping. Mallory slid up the wall, peering through the gap between the curtain and the sill. A large man with a long, white beard and flowing hair swayed against the wall, using one hand to steady himself while he tapped a metal pole with a forked end onto the ground.

'Liquid gold is what we need, yeah liquid gold come to me.' The words rolled and lifted while he tapped the ground. She couldn't tell for sure whether he was drunk, or caught in a trance, but she didn't like his chances of getting water, oil or any other kind of gold out of the pavement. She watched him continue his ritual along the wall of the building, until he went around the corner. She went back to bed, staring at the first rays of morning light coming through the curtains, as the strange calls of the birds of central Australia heralded the breaking dawn.

Soft light spread above the subterranean dwellers in underground dugouts, the locals in aboveground workers' cottages and the 'out-of-towners' in hotel rooms who couldn't face sleeping in the darkness below. Those who slept below-ground were cocooned in the cool, blanketing darkness of their chosen caves. They slumbered, unaware of the clear skies above them, or the birds wheeling and crying in tumultuous upper thermals. They continued to dream, ignorant to the heated winds on the plains to the east chasing red dust toward the town and casting an ochre haze across the lower expanse of the sky. Oblivious to the angry, black clouds gathering from the opposite direction.

Mallory tossed and turned on her bed. The pressure to move became unbearable. She had a whole day to kill in a one-horse town where she would stand out just by hanging around doing nothing. She picked up the tourist pamphlets she'd collected from the foyer. Camel rides, plane rides, opal mining and guided tours into the desert. Being trapped on a guided tour with no control over planning, transportation or supplies, was her worst nightmare. Visiting any of the main attractions in town might cause

18

somebody to remember her, and she wasn't going near any stinky, horrible camels.

On her last holiday in Turkey with her father, he'd decided it would be a great idea to book a camel trek and thought it was hilarious when one of them spat on her. Of course, it was the one she had to ride. It kept looking backwards at her for the entire trek, as though aware of her dislike. When they reached their destination, it refused to sit to let her off for almost twenty minutes. The handler became angry and made her change camels. The new camel didn't like her either. It bolted home when they were close to finishing the ride. The handlers ran after the wayward animal, screaming instructions at Mallory in Turkish. All she could do was cling to the 'saddle' until the beast came to a halt. An argument ensued between her father and the handlers. They insisted she was possessed by the Devil and had ruined their best camel. Her father felt that the opposite was true. She couldn't remember how the argument ended, but she sure enough knew she would not get on an uncooperative, ugly camel ever again!

She dropped the camel expedition pamphlet in the bin, and pushed the memories of her father away. He'd been missing for so long. It was hard to maintain faith that he would ever be found. She wished she could escape, ride her motorbike to the Painted Desert. Perhaps stop and take pictures of the famous dingo fence, maybe take a walk on the Moon Plain. She flicked through the remaining flyers, looking for inspiration. It was tempting to take a plane trip to Lake Eyre, get the lie of the land before Wednesday, but it wouldn't do to be seen out and about. There was too much risk involved. She pushed the remaining pamphlets toward the back of the tiny desk, resigning herself to the boredom of the hotel. As she did, she noticed a small envelope propped behind the hotel menu. Her eyes widened at the spidery script on the front. She grabbed a pair of gloves from her bag and broke the seal on the envelope with shaking hands.

Mallory's hand flew to her mouth as she read the note. It wasn't possible; had to be a set up! She stared around the room, almost expecting Jimmy the Cat, or perhaps Derek, to appear out of nowhere. She paced the room, struggling with the temptation in the note. It was important to stay out of sight, but if the note was for real? It meant that someone out there had information about her father. She hesitated a moment longer, her mind on the unlikely confluence of herself, Derek and Jimmy in the same desert at the very bottom of the world. Every instinct told her that the note was dangerous, but the need to find her father was stronger than common sense.

She slipped on a pair of jeans and t-shirt, before contemplating her image in the mirror. Disguise was her best defence. She rarely went out looking like her natural self. She looked into her violet eyes, so startling against her pale skin and curls, and wondered if she should cover them with contacts, but surely this day was the best time to be herself. She would be able to observe the informant without fear of detection in the desert.

She checked her rucksack for supplies of dehydrated food, water and a basic first aid kit, and packed extra water before slinging it onto her back. When she reached her bike, she double-checked her tools and puncture-kit before taking to the road.

Mornings were the best time of day to Mallory, when the burdens of yesterday could be removed and the new day came loaded with possibilities and hope. When she reached the outskirts of town, she gunned the bike north, roaring along the empty highway at an exhilarating speed.

Coober Pedy disappeared like a desert mirage behind her, and the country in front opened into an expanse of ochres, creams and yellows, like none she had ever seen before. The landscape was as close to sublime as she had ever witnessed, and she enjoyed the rare freedom of an empty highway and country devoid of humanity. The isolation encouraged her mind to wander as she raced into the encroaching day, so that the Roadhouse at Mount Willoughby appeared more quickly than she expected. She pulled into the car park and looked around before taking off her helmet. It consisted of the same red dust and lack of vegetation, as the streets in Coober Pedy. She scanned the verandah, suddenly aware that she'd taken to the road without a disguise. She knew her true identity was safe, but she still preferred to keep it shrouded. She grinned at the thought of the mug shots Interpol posted—even her family would have trouble recognising her. She scanned the carpark beside the hotel. There were no cars in sight and no tour buses from town. It was extremely unlikely that she would meet anyone out here.

She climbed the steps into the cool shade of the verandah, ordered a hearty breakfast, and settled with a coffee and map of the area. She traced the line of the road through the Painted Desert to Arckaringa Station and back down to Coober Pedy. Coming from the opposite direction was surely the best way to get to the meeting place without being observed by the informant. It would also keep her out of trouble and out of sight, until tomorrow. A long ride, easily nine hours, then back to her room like any other weary tourist to rest and relax.

A white 4WD skidded to a halt in front of the roadhouse, sending a pall of dust across the verandah. She coughed, flicked the map and glared at the offending vehicle and its occupant. The driver stepped out, taking the steps two at a time, before jumping onto the verandah. He was tall and lean with caramel skin, and revealed a head of thick, black hair when he took off his hat.

'Sorry miss, I didn't see you sitting there.' He smiled all the way to his brilliant green eyes and Mallory's pulse zinged.

He started to speak again when the door flung open.

A heavyset woman ran toward him. 'Sam Walker, you bastard. What the hell are you doing here?' She grabbed him in a bear hug, almost lifting him off the floor despite his height.

'Hey good to see you too, Annie,' he laughed.

'And that no-good dad of yours, when is he coming back this way?'

'He's at the Breakaways, so who knows.'

Mallory tried to concentrate on the map, but the stranger's voice, that perfect blend of depth and musicality, was divine. The verandah fell silent. She looked up from the map to find him standing at her table again.

'Hey, it's boring eating breakfast alone. Do you mind if I join you?'

She was surprised at how easy he made it appear, to just walk up and invite yourself to a person's table. She nodded, dropping her eyes to the map while she regained her composure.

'Do you always read maps upside down?'

She focused on the map, her neck and face burning bright red. 'No, it's a skill I've just developed.'

He laughed. She looked up quickly, but there was no malice in his face. He looked happy to be alive. That was a look she hadn't seen on many people.

When her breakfast arrived, he nodded at her plate. 'Tuck in. Mine won't be far behind. My name's Sam, by the way.'

'Oh yes, I'm Amanda Anderson.'

'Pleased to meet you, Amanda Anderson.' He held out his hand.

She put down her cutlery, flustered all over again as she reached across the table to shake his hand.

His fingers were long and sensitive, his palms looked soft. A pianist's hand perhaps, or possibly an artist? She placed her hand in his, unaware that her day was about to get bent out of shape.

When his skin touched hers, every nerve-end came alive in a fabulous burst of crazy energy. The hairs on her body rose and goose bumps raced across her skin. Tingling erupted from the nape of her neck down to her feet. She stared at him in a daze, wondering if he was feeling it too, but he chatted with her hand still in his, as though nothing had happened, and it was the most ordinary thing in the world to sit down with a stranger and hold onto her hand before breakfast. She withdrew her hand reluctantly. The coldness of the cutlery on her skin was painful after the heat of his touch.

Sam's breakfast arrived. They ate in companionable silence until a black and white dog sidled under the table, sniffing for scraps. It dropped on its haunches near Mallory to scratch behind its ear. She watched in horror as dust and hair spread like a toxic cloud toward the table.

Sam stomped his foot. 'Get off, Boofhead. You know better than to be on the verandah.'

The dog skulked down the steps, giving Sam one last wounded look, before disappearing into the shade beneath the floorboards.

'You seem quite at home here,' Mallory observed.

He nodded. 'Yeah, I rarely get a chance to visit now, but my dad and mum always stopped here on their way to Coober Pedy when I was a kid. Dad and Annie go a long way back. I always got spoilt rotten. Ice cream, jelly – I could have whatever I wanted. The place seemed like heaven on a stick to me.'

'It's funny isn't it, how the places your parents took you when you were a kid stay in your memory, and kind of sad how they don't live up to expectations when you're grown.' The words shocked her as they came out of her mouth. She didn't understand how this man, who she had only just met, could make her drop her guard so completely.

He busied himself with his bacon and eggs and didn't reply. She felt sure he was measuring her words, judging her moment of weakness.

'I guess I'm lucky in that respect. I still have Annie to keep the deception alive,' he said, his voice soft with understanding. 'Because the thing that made those places special, is the love offered by the adults that were with you.'

She ducked her head, aware of a sudden lump in her throat. Her thoughts flew to her father. It was entirely possible she might burst into tears and make a complete fool of herself. She glanced at her watch. This man, who she had known for less than an hour, was having a devastating effect on her.

She placed her cutlery on her plate. 'I have to go. It was really nice to meet you.'

Sam grinned. 'Right. Nice.'

Sam remained on the verandah long after her departure, staring in the direction she had taken. Annie came out to the verandah and stood beside him, raising her eyebrows when he looked down at her.

He sighed. 'What?'

She pointed at two eskies inside the door, and then nodded toward the road. 'You don't need me to tell you, son.'

***

Out on the highway, Mallory shook her head, the hollow words; *it was really nice to meet you*, reverberating in her head until they lost all meaning. She cursed, wondering why she couldn't extricate herself from social situations with grace. If she could only turn around, go back to him, tell him that he had reminded her how good human touch could feel, and how easy some connections could be. But such thoughts were pointless. She was here to do a job and get out of the country with a pretty gem, and her life.

She forced her thoughts back to her solo day trip, her mind on the impending rendezvous. The landscape seemed blasted and desolate, a good match for her current state of mind. After two hours she finally reached a deserted picnic area on the side of the never-ending road leading back to Coober Pedy. She stretched her legs and admired a flush of colourful desert flowers in the dunes beyond the car park. So strange to see so much living colour in such a dry place. As she rummaged through her backpack for a snack, she heard a vehicle approaching from the direction of Mount Willoughby. She pulled a drink out of her bag and waited near her bike until the car came into view. Always good to be the watcher in an isolated spot, and never a good idea to walk away from the only transport you had.

A white 4WD geared down as it approached the rest area. Mallory's heart did a little skip of excitement. It looked like Sam's vehicle. Her pulse leapt at the thought. She would see him again, ask him questions that had come to her when she was on the road and perhaps even feel his hand on her skin once again. The 4WD rolled under trees at the far end of the rest stop. She held her breath. After what seemed an eternity, a woman alighted, lifting a hand in an offhand wave to Mallory, before heading toward the public toilets.

She started to breathe again. It was stupid to expect him to cross her path again. Most likely he'd already forgotten she existed. She grabbed her bag and walked toward the flowers drifting through the red dunes, stomping her disappointment into the desert sand, determined to put the disturbing stranger out of her mind. She stopped when she reached her goal. The Poached-egg Daisies looked exactly as their name suggested, and the delicate hollyhocks and sea heaths were like beacons of hope in the desolate landscape. If these fragile flowers could flourish in such an arid environment, surely anything was possible.

The sound of a motor roaring to life broke the silence. The woman in the white 4WD tooted the horn and flung a careless hand out the window as she drove onto the highway. Mallory stared at the empty carpark. The contact was over an hour late. Her earlier suspicions returned, and her fragile hope of discovering her father's location withered.

When she returned to her bike, she finished her water and refilled at the rainwater tank in the rest area. The heat was already unbearable, making her lightweight t-shirt cling and her jeans burn her legs. She wiped a cloth over her face, applied sunscreen and surveyed the stunted saltbush around the rest area. This desert reminded her of the time she went on vacation with her father to Desert Hot Springs in California. He had always loved hot, lightly populated areas. A reaction perhaps, to growing up in Northern England, and facing the insular necessities of Canadian winters after he married her mother.

She was fourteen at the time of the vacation; argumentative, sassy, bored and angry at her parents for separating. She winced now, to remember how she fought him at every step, telling him she hated the landscape, hated the hot springs, hated him. She could still see the pain in his eyes after her outburst. Still hear him reminding her that he would always love her no matter what, that life was too short to hate. It was a thing he had always said, that life was too short to hate, wait or arrive late. Shame coursed through her when she thought about the beautiful hotel he had booked and the activities he arranged. Of course, he was right; life had indeed proven to be too short. He disappeared a month after their holiday, and had been missing for twelve years. She'd been trying hard to make her own life count for something ever since.

She swallowed, pushing back the tears that threatened to engulf her. Her mother was pragmatic, said it was time to accept that Dad was gone, but Mallory felt certain he was out there somewhere, maybe thinking of her right now, wondering how she was doing. She closed her eyes, focusing on the way his blue eyes used to dance when he told jokes, the aromas of sweet rum and cigars when he was at home. The way his hands flashed and weaved when he spoke, as though they were knitting together the less believable elements of his tall tales. She cast back further, remembering how the tickle of his beard on her face at bedtime, the hum of central heating, the late-night clink of ice in tumblers and the deep rumble of his voice, formed the security blanket of her childhood nights. It was important to keep those small details alive, to keep him alive in her memory until he was found. If she let it all go, let him go, there would be no imagining him back into her life. Harder to imagine a reunion, though. What would he make of the woman his daughter had become? She was certain she'd made mistakes beyond the understanding of a consummate professional like her father. She hoped he would be proud that she'd chosen to follow in his footsteps.

She packed her rucksack, conducted one last check on her bike, and stared up and down the empty road. A sudden thought hit her. Perhaps whoever left the note in her room wanted her out of Coober Pedy for the day. The futility of waiting any longer at the deserted stop hit her. She swung her leg over the bike and gunned the engine. Once on the road, she pushed thoughts of her father away and gave in to the soporific sameness of the miles spinning away beneath her wheels. The bike travelled smoothly and she made good time until a loud bang sounded. The back of the bike kicked and wobbled with enough force to make her apply all of her experience to keep control.

She came to a halt on the side of the road and knew before she looked that the back tyre had blown. Mending a puncture was easy, but the rim was a different matter. She lifted the seat of the bike, pulled out a roll of tools and looked at the sky. The sun was just past noon. She had plenty of time. She wrapped a handkerchief around her neck and got to work. Sweat poured down her back, legs and arms. The heat radiating off the metal components of the bike made her aware that time was her enemy out here. She had to get the bike on the road as quickly as possible, but the worst thing to do was panic. She worked methodically, giving the puncture her complete attention, until the sound of a vehicle approaching from the direction of Coober Pedy made her pause.

A beaten-up Landcruiser with a thick film of red dust covering the original colour slowed as it approached. She kept working, hoping the occupants would see she was okay and leave her in peace, but she could already hear that her hopes wouldn't be answered. She stood, wiping her hands on her jeans as the vehicle pulled up beside her. When she saw a heavyset, bearded man her heart sank. She hated these awkward encounters with well-meaning older men, often with less mechanical experience than she possessed, who insisted on 'helping'. There never seemed to be a way to deflect them without causing offence.

The man leant a meaty arm on the window sill. 'You right love?'

She nodded. He looked down the length of her, as though weighing her for market, and grinned before wiping a hand across the back of his mouth. 'Yeah, you look alright to me.'

The muscles in her stomach coiled. Her eyes slid to the open seat of the bike. She saw the Glock, tucked safely in its pouch, and took a deep breath to offset the wave of adrenalin hitting her system.

He put his shoulder into the driver's door. The metal gave a tortured screech as it opened. His blue singlet was stained black with sweat, his shorts rode down displaying a muscular torso. Despite his size, he moved lightly. 'You're kind of handy, eh?'

She nodded and moved toward the bike, her hand tightening on the spanner.

He stepped closer, glancing at her hand and smiled, revealing broken teeth. 'Don't have much to say. I like that in a lady.'

Mallory watched him; her stomach clenched now into a solid knot. She would have to neutralise him, but then what? She hadn't finished working on the bike.

His smile kept spreading, looking more like a snarl when his lips finally stretched to their limit. 'I'll help ya finish, yeah.'

He turned and walked toward the back of the Landcruiser. She relaxed, wondering if she'd misread the situation as he swung open the back door of the car. All she could see were his boots and bare legs near the vehicle, but something about his movements seemed wrong. She went to the bike and grabbed a screwdriver, pushing it into the pocket of her trousers.

He stepped away from the back of the Landcruiser with a sawn-off shotgun in his hands, and nodded toward his vehicle. 'I've been sent by the First Lady. Get in.'

A spurt of adrenalin coursed through her body, making her heart and head pound and her pulse skitter. The heat intensified and the colours around her were so bright they hurt. His movements were exaggerated as he walked toward her, as though she were watching a slow-motion documentary about a predator going in for the kill.

When she didn't move, his eyes narrowed. 'I knew I'd find you along the road – where are you gonna go out here? Now, play the game and you won't get hurt.'

She read the empty violence in his eyes and knew she wouldn't leave this desert if she got into the car with him. She stepped back, but his arm snaked out with surprising speed, grabbing her by the wrist, jerking her off balance. She leapt at him, intent on using his grip as a counter balance. His balance slipped for a moment and she thrust backwards, reaching toward the open seat of the bike. He came after her and slammed the butt of the rifle into the side of her head, making stars explode behind her eyes. Her hand flung out, knocking the bike seat down. As she dropped to the ground, she heard the sound of an insistent horn, as though someone was playing the trumpet, and wondered if her ears were damaged by the blow. He dragged her toward the car. She fought back, but her arms and legs felt like lead as he lifted her off the ground and threw her over his shoulder.

He laughed. 'The First Lady told me you'd put up a fight.'

Her head spun. *Who was the First Lady? Why would an unknown woman want her dead? And how did she know her father?* She lost consciousness as the trumpeting sound grew louder and turned into a deafening explosion.

3

SOMETHING cold and dark covered her face. Her head throbbed like a drum. She let her senses expand, trying to visualise her environment. She was lying on a soft surface. She placed a palm downwards. Warm vinyl with stitching; probably the backseat of the man's Landcruiser. The vehicle wasn't moving. She listened, couldn't hear him breathing. He must be out of the cab, doing whatever it was cold-blooded killers did in their spare time. *God! Now was not the time to make cynical jokes!* She kept her breathing even, tried to stay calm. Her arms were not restrained. She moved them tentatively, feeling for the screwdriver in her pocket. It was gone, of course. No surprise that he hadn't bothered to restrain her – there was nowhere to run, or hide. She put a hand to the side of her head and frowned. What kind of killer bandaged victims? Footsteps approached the vehicle. She put her arm back by her side. Her only hope was the element of surprise.

The door opened. She felt him lean over her. 'Amanda? Can you hear me?'

The voice was familiar, and far from frightening. She frowned, trying to cut through her fog of confusion. Had

31

the man in the desert been a nightmare?

A warm hand took hers, bringing memories of her breakfast companion flooding back. 'Sam?'

He took the flannel off her face, smiling into her eyes. 'Thank Christ you're alright.'

'What happened? How did I get here?'

'Lucky I came along when I did.'

'But he had a gun. And I heard an explosion.'

He opened an esky on the floor of the vehicle and pressed a cold pack to the side of her head. 'Don't know about that. When he saw me coming, he took off.' He didn't look at her. 'He took off fast. Did you happen to get a number plate?' he asked.

'No. I was too busy trying to survive.'

'Yes, of course. What did he look like?'

She noticed the determined interest beneath his casual tone. 'Why? Are you going to arrest him when you're done nursing me?'

He laughed. 'Nah, that's one for the coppers.'

'Well, let me think. He was a big guy, easy two hundred and twenty pounds, but fit. Aged around fifty with salt and pepper beard and hair, brown eyes and sun-damaged skin. Wearing a blue singlet and shorts. He had a tattoo of a naked woman in a kneeling position with a noose around her neck on his left wrist.'

He looked at her in admiration. 'Wow, that's pretty good recall for a girl who's just been hit on the head.'

'It's a habit I picked up from my dad. He was big on observation.'

He perched on the edge of the seat, studying her face while she spoke. The chemistry she felt at the roadhouse returned. Butterflies multiplied in her stomach and fluttered up her spine. He studied her for so long after she finished speaking, she wondered if he intended to kiss her, and immediately dismissed the idea as stupid. The hit to her head must have been solid!

The sound of a truck on the road broke the spell. She

felt relief and disappointment course through her as he climbed out of the 4WD and flagged the driver down.

'I thought these roads were supposed to be bloody deserted,' she muttered.

'Sam! What you doing out here, mate?' the driver called out.

'Hey, Joey, good to see you! I'm helping a traveller out. I need a quick favour,' Sam said.

Mallory sat up, her head doing slow, sickening spins. She saw Sam disappear into the cabin of the truck and wondered if there was anyone out here in the middle of nowhere that he didn't know.

Inside the truck, Sam gave a quick account of her misadventure and wrote down the description of the tattooed man. 'Do you know anyone around here with a tattoo like that?'

Joey shook his head. 'Nah, he's gotta be a blow-in.'

Sam looked around the cab and nodded to a box filled with water bottles in the sleeping compartment. 'Can I take a bottle?' he asked as he opened the door. 'And can you radio that through to the police at Coober Pedy and Alice Springs, please.'

'Sure mate, but why can't you?'

'Not possible right now.'

After the truck pulled away, Sam returned to the car. He held up the bottle of water. 'Joey gave us some extra water,' he explained unnecessarily. 'I finished fixing your tyre while you were sleeping,' he continued. 'Couldn't put the tools away, though. The seat is locked. There's a rest area about ten kilometres up the road. It has shade and running water. We can have lunch there. I'll ride your bike there if you think you're well enough to drive my car.'

Mallory's thoughts flew to the Glock. She fished the bike key out of her pocket, her expression neutral. 'No, I'm good to ride thanks.'

The deserted rest area, with its small clump of trees shading a picnic table, pit toilet and bore water, looked inviting after the heat of the road. Mallory nosed the vehicle under the trees and turned off the motor. Sam pulled in behind her and opened the back of the 4WD, pulling out two eskies and dumping them on the table.

'What's all this?' she asked.

He laughed. 'Annie never lets me leave empty-handed. I have enough food here for five people.'

His face lit up as he spoke about the woman at the roadhouse. The sight of his generous smile made warm tingles run up her back, and she forgot to ask why he needed water from Joey when there were plenty in the eskies. She enjoyed watching him while he laughed, talked and placed the food on the table. The aroma of roast chicken made her realise she was hungry.

She looked at her watch, shocked to discover it was already past two. 'How far are we from Coober Pedy?' she asked.

'About three and half hours,' he said.

She did a quick calculation. She could have lunch and get back just after dark. She relaxed, intending to enjoy the meal and the company after the horror of the morning.

As if reading her mind, Sam said, 'You're doing amazing for what you've been through. How are you feeling?'

She started to formulate an evasive answer and stopped. He deserved better after what he'd done for her. 'Right now, I'm okay, but I'm already having flashbacks.' She shivered. 'I figure I'll probably have them for a while. And, while we're on the subject, thank you for saving my life.'

He nodded. 'It's a typical reaction, you know. I'm having flashbacks too. I just keep thanking God I arrived when I did.'

A powerful memory of the tattooed man hit her like a body blow. She was back on the side of the road with his hot breath scorching her shoulder, his hand crushing her wrist, his body towering over her as he dragged her toward his vehicle. The logical chain of events that would have followed leapt into her mind in technicolour detail. Tears sprang to her eyes, and she let out a small whimper.

Sam jumped up, gathering her into his arms. 'It's alright, let it out,' he said.

The full force of her near miss hit home. She realised for the first time in her life that she wasn't self-sufficient, and would be dead, or no doubt wish she was right now, if this man hadn't been in the right place at the right time.

She let herself sink against him, sobbing her pent-up shock into his chest. He hugged her without speaking, allowing her to work through her emotions in her own time. When she calmed down, she marvelled at his ability to be supportive without invading her need for privacy.

He pulled a clean napkin off the table and handed it to her. She took it, blowing her nose with gusto, stopping with embarrassment at the honking sound she made.

She giggled, and he laughed, hugging her close. 'Now that's what I call getting it all out of your system.'

They settled at the table to eat before the clouds of flies and persistent ants carried the food away.

She brushed at the pesky insects. 'To think I thought this desert was devoid of all life forms this morning,' she exclaimed.

'There's plenty here if you know how to look. When we've finished eating, I'll give you a quick lesson on tracking if you're interested.'

'Wow, yes please.'

He spent the meal pointing in different directions at distant, barely visible landmarks, explaining their importance to the traditional owners of the land. She was amazed at the depth of his knowledge. If she were asked to describe Canada, she knew she couldn't begin to give such a nuanced account. Sure, she could tell him about the cold and the snow, the forests and the incredible natural beauty, but everything she would say was right there to be seen without her telling. He revealed a hidden country within the dry, red dunes and grey soaks that were visible to her. He introduced her to a land of treasures and mysteries, made her realise that she'd been walking through the desert with her eyes half-closed.

When they finished eating, he pointed toward a soak near the road. 'If you're feeling okay, I'll grab you a hat and show you some tracks.'

She nodded and followed him to the car, taking the hat he offered. They set off toward the soak. He stopped almost immediately and dropped on his haunches. 'See here. An old man goanna, this one. A good size and not in any hurry when he came through this way.'

She looked at the faint marks on the ground. They could have belonged to a bird or a lizard, as far as she could see. How could he be so sure of what he saw?

Sam pointed along the barely visible trail. 'See here where his tail dragged to the side, and look, he stopped and tasted the air just there.' He jumped up like a small boy on an adventure, following signs on the ground. He stopped and pointed at dark pellets on the ground near the edge of the soak. 'Wallaby scats.'

When the pair drew close to the soak, lizards and birds darted into the stunted, shrubby plants growing around its edges.

'Hey look at the little beauties,' he cried, when a wave of budgerigars rose from the water's edge. They flashed blue, yellow and green against the red dunes, chattering into the sky before swooping back above them to land in shrubs on the other side of the soak.

Sam stood beside her, following the flight path of the birds, as if he had never seen them before. After they landed, he touched her arm. 'Look there, under that ledge. That's a Perentie lizard.'

'I can't believe how much wildlife is here!'

'This area is home to kangaroos, wallabies, emu and plenty of lizards and snakes. It also has eagles and parrots, even the odd black swan and pelican when there's a wet passing through.'

'What's a wet?'

'Big rain. Doesn't happen often, but when it does, the desert comes alive with wildflowers and birds. The birds know how to track the weather. They get here quick smart.'

'How do you know so much?' she asked.

'My old man grew up on this land. He taught me, and his old man taught him. When the time comes, I'll teach my kids.'

Mallory stopped breathing. The chemistry between them was so strong, it simply hadn't occurred to her he might be married with a family. She went hot and cold all at once, keeping her face still while he talked about the importance of sharing knowledge with the next generation.

She wished she were alone, so she could lament her own stupidity and put her hormones back where they belonged. She should have known he wouldn't be single.

They walked to the other side of the soak. She tried to stay attentive while he showed her the minute differences between bird prints, but her thoughts kept drifting back to his touch, and the fact that he was a married man.

He stopped mid-sentence, tilting her hat so he could see her face. 'I think I've lost you. You feeling okay?'

She took the opportunity to escape. 'No, I should go back.'

'Of course. I was wrong to keep you out here so long.'

The walk, and the visceral disappointment she was experiencing, drained her. When they reached the shade, she dropped onto the bench, resting her head on her knees. Sam appeared, squatting in front of her with water.

His look of concern made her thoughts return to her father and all of the long years he had been missing. Would things have been different if she hadn't waited for him to break the silence all those years ago? If she'd swallowed her pride and asked why he wouldn't talk to her in the two weeks before he disappeared? Would he have given her a clue, some hint she could have deciphered to find him? His silence was so out of character, but she'd been too wrapped in herself, had imagined everything was about her. He always said he didn't have time to hate, wait or be late, but she let her petty emotions get in the way; let far too much time go by without questioning, until it was too late to discover the truth.

She decided she would not leave Sam without knowing for sure if he was married. 'How old are your children?'

He looked at her, his expression blank. She experienced a moment of panic, imagining he'd seen straight through her question, to the sexual desire below.

'Umm, I don't have kids. What gave you that idea?'

Her heart lifted, but her mind was quick to take control. He might not have kids, but he was probably about to start a family. 'Oh, I thought you said you had children.'

He shook his head. 'Nah. I meant someday. When I meet the right girl and all that, you know.' He coloured, looking boyish as he spoke.

Mallory wanted to jump up and down and holler for joy. Instead, she took the water, keeping her eyes on the horizon while she drank. He wasn't married, and he hadn't met the right girl! Excitement raged through her, so powerful it surprised her. She realised she wanted him terribly and wondered if her recent encounter with Derek was responsible for the way her hormones were currently rampaging through her body. She passed the empty cup to him and their fingers touched. She looked up at him, her breath catching.

He bent down, lifting her off the bench. Her heart skipped at the naked question in his eyes. She leant toward him, all thoughts of the past and future wiped as his arms encircled her. Their lips touched, and the world fell away. She melted into him, wrapping her arms around his neck, pushing her fingers into his hair. His breathing accelerated as he ran a hand down her back, pulling her body closer to his. She moaned, her own breath coming in gasps when the hard contours of his body pressed against hers. He kissed her neck and shoulders. Then he was holding her face between his hands, kissing her softly. She opened her eyes, staring into his.

He stopped kissing her, kept her face between his hands, stroking her cheek as he spoke. 'Christ, I'm not sure what just happened.'

'Same.'

He let go of her and sat down on the bench. Her legs shook as she sat beside him. She needed to touch him, to feel the silky pressure of his skin on hers.

His fingers closed around hers. 'I hope you don't think this is my normal behaviour.'

She smiled. 'Ditto.'

'Bit stupid of me, though. After what you've been through today.'

She smiled again. 'Don't worry, you're good with me.'

'Thanks.'

His answering smile sent shivers down her spine. God, he didn't know just how good he was with her. She wanted to kiss him again, right now; wanted to remove every item he was wearing so she could slide her hands all over his muscular body. She wanted to find out how deep the fire in him ran. Her pulse hopped. She pulled her thoughts to a halt. The excitement she felt, just thinking about him, was like nothing she had ever experienced before. If she didn't watch out, she'd be panting all over him.

He looked toward the horizon. 'Hey, you better get started if you're heading to Coober Pedy today.' He pointed to a bank of low-hanging black clouds. 'You'll miss that storm if you go now.'

She followed his hand. He was right. If she didn't hurry, she'd ride into a storm at dusk, when the risk of collisions with kangaroos was high.

'Where are you headed?' she asked.

'Not sure yet.'

She frowned into the empty landscape. There didn't seem to be a huge choice of destinations out here, but then, he'd already shown her the error of that kind of thinking. It was quite likely he knew someone who would give him a bed for the night. *Perhaps a woman?*

She stood up, shaking away her thoughts. She'd just met the guy and already she was wondering if he had another woman tucked away! She waited, hoping he'd stand and take her in his arms again, but he remained seated, seemed absorbed with the ground between his boots.

'Well, this is goodbye I guess,' she said awkwardly.

'Yeah.'

She waited, but he didn't move. Anger started to move inside her. *Surely what they just experienced was worth another kiss?* She walked to her bike, taking her time in case he decided to relent, come after her. She watched him out of the corner of her eye. He sat with his head hanging between his shoulders, his gaze still on the ground between his boots. If he didn't want to acknowledge her, she had no intention of hanging around like a lovesick teenager.

She roared out of the carpark without looking back, cursing her own stupidity. The time she spent with him had seemed so singular. The sexual chemistry, amazing. It hadn't occurred to her that he might not feel the same way. She cursed, trying to hold hard to her anger, but after the events of the day, it was no use. Tears streamed down her cheeks.

***

The ride back to Coober Pedy passed largely unnoticed by Mallory. Her mind whirled with thoughts of Sam. Despite the anger she felt, she couldn't believe she had ever felt real sexual chemistry before today. He was so different to anyone she knew. The immediate connection she experienced when he looked at her on the verandah at the roadhouse was still with her, as if his DNA had been etched into hers. Recalling every word he said to her, every gesture, and the kiss they finally shared, was an exquisite torture she didn't want to stop. It felt as though her body had been waiting for him all of her life; as though it knew something she couldn't begin to understand.

She wanted to turn around and ride back, wanted to ask him if he would take her in his arms and kiss her one more time, but it was obvious the connection wasn't shared. Whatever his reasons for kissing her, he hadn't felt what she did. All she could hope was that the passion within her would fade, but as soon as she had the thought, she knew it was false. She would have trouble forgetting how he'd made her feel.

She turned her thoughts away from Sam, focusing instead on why she was in Australia. She couldn't afford to let an outback playboy distract her from the job at hand. And there was also the mystery of her attacker. Who was the First Lady? And why did she lure Mallory into the desert with promises of information about her father? Whoever it was knew that she was here to get the Virgin Rainbow. The mystery of the woman would have to wait as well. She couldn't afford to get distracted. She had to deliver the opal to Trafford. She knew why Trafford had picked her and Derek to do the job. They were a good team. Her ability to read people and stay calm under pressure was complemented by his logical thinking and technological savvy. Trafford always picked the best team for his jobs, because failure was not in his dictionary. If she let anything, or anyone, ruin this mission, her life would be on the line.

Mallory slowed the bike as she entered the outskirts of Coober Pedy. The recent rain made the streets sparkle under the early evening lights. The smell of damp, and the moisture darkened buildings and roads, made the town seem like a different place. For a start, there were more people on the streets than she'd seen since she arrived. It seemed the rain had the power to flush everything out into the open when it came inland.

She parked the bike in the long shadows behind the hotel and decided to keep her helmet on until she reached the back entrance. As she stepped into the darkened cove, an arm curled around her, dragging her backwards. Corded muscles crushed her throat, and memories of the earlier events of the day sent her into a panic, quickly replaced by anger at the thought of another stranger attempting to harm her. Instead of going backwards with the pressure, she pushed forward until her assailant resisted, then let herself go, using the other person's weight to propel both of them backwards into the brick wall behind, slamming her helmet into her aggressor's head as she did.

'Jesus, shit!' yelped Derek.

She turned around. He was bent over with blood pouring out of his nose.

'What are you playing at, you idiot?'

He straightened up, pressing fingers to his nose. 'Christ, I just wanted to remind you to be on your guard, but I can see I had no reason to worry.'

Mallory snorted as she took her helmet off. 'You dick! Why would you do that?'

His eyes widened at the bandage around her head. 'What happened to you?'

'I had a bit of an accident on the road.'

He raised a doubtful eyebrow. 'Hope you didn't draw attention to yourself.'

'Look, I'm tired and sore. I don't care what you hope. Is there anything you actually want, Derek?'

His gaze ran up and down her body. He whistled. 'I forgot how good you are at disguises. You are still looking rather lovely, and it is so terribly boring here.' His eyes softened as he stepped toward her. 'As a matter of fact, you're looking incredibly hot, Mal. What do you think? Perhaps we could try again?' He touched her cheek, smiling at her with his velvet blue eyes. 'Or at least, we could have some fun, for old time's sake?'

She hesitated. Perhaps Derek was exactly the distraction she needed to forget everything that had happened in the desert today. An image of Sam explaining the importance of the country and its landmarks returned. He had such fire and integrity, and there was no denying that the rhythm of his speech and the beat of his pulse had entered her veins. Just thinking about him brought back the feel of his hands on her body. A slow burn ran through her thighs when she remembered his lips on hers.

'Thanks for the offer,' she said. 'But I'll pass.'

Derek stepped back as though slapped. 'But hang on, babe —'

She stepped past him, no longer interested in what he had to offer. Aware she was not in disguise, she stopped in an alcove and waited until the hotel clerk left the desk. When she reached her room, she peeled off her leathers, dropped onto the bed, and let the memory of Sam's hands and soft kisses return.

***

Derek left the car park, sauntering down a side alley to keep to the backstreets, before turning onto Hutchison Street. He wondered if he were taking precautions for no reason, because he had not seen Jimmy the Cat in town. Mallory was paranoid. She didn't seem to be the same girl he remembered. She had always been soft and accommodating when they were together, ready to go along with whatever he suggested. Now she was cold and edgy. He ran their conversation over in his head and decided she must be getting too old for this game. He wasn't sure he liked her very much anymore.

A group of women walked toward him, their heels

clacking on the cement. Each one looked him up and down. He smiled and winked at a slim blonde in the middle. The others giggled and elbowed each other as he passed.

'We'll be at the Outback Bar, and we'll be looking for you, handsome,' one of them called to him.

It was that easy. Good humour restored, he walked with a spring in his step toward his room.

Across the road, a dark figure glided along the footpath, shifting in and out of the early evening pedestrians and doorways like a wraith. Every time Derek stopped, the figure slowed, flanking him until he reached his hotel.

After he went inside, Jimmy the Cat stepped out of the shadows opposite. Pedestrians encountering him gave the silent, unmoving man a wide berth, as if unconsciously aware of the threat he posed.

4

THE alarm shrilled over and over, the noise chasing Mallory along subterranean corridors. She ran for her life, taking a left into a dead end. Turning and running, she searched for the main corridor. She saw it ahead, was almost on her way to freedom when Jimmy the Cat appeared. He held out his hand, revealing a large Bowie knife. It flashed under the fluorescent lights as he closed the gap between them with feline grace. She felt for her Glock. It was gone. The alarm was insistent, drilling into her panicked brain. Jimmy closed in with the knife, leaping, grabbing her hair, spinning her body, pulling her head back until she screamed from the pain. He drove his knee into her back and raised the knife, plunging it toward her throat...

She sat bolt upright, sweaty. Her head throbbed under the bandage, and the alarm shrilled. Her body shook in the darkness while she tried to work out where she was. The bed! She was safe in the bed in her hotel room.

The alarm! It was the phone, ringing in the darkness. She flailed around, fear coursing through her veins, making her clumsy. It was only a horrible dream, probably brought on by her encounter with the nasty freak in the desert. A glass fell to the floor and the obligatory hotel Bible went flying while she tried to locate the braying instrument on the bedside table. She picked it up, savouring the silence for a second, before saying hello.

'Miss Anderson? You have a visitor.'

'What?'

'Mr Sam Walker is waiting in the foyer for you.'

Sam here, now, why, how? He was the last person she expected, after the way they parted. A momentary tingle of suspicion raised the hairs on her arms. *How had he found her? Why was he here? What could he possibly want from her?* It hadn't even occurred to her that he might also come to Coober Pedy. The thought of him taking the time to track her down was exciting, but it was worrying too, how quickly and easily she could be found by a stranger in a foreign land. What's more, what was she supposed to do with him, now he had found her? She couldn't go out in public, not tonight. It was too risky. But it was surely too forward to invite him to her room? But then, she might never see him again, and she wanted to have – she stopped mid-thought. *As if she needed to worry about any of it now! He wasn't exactly falling over himself to say goodbye when they parted.* She stared at the wall, her mind in turmoil until the clerk's concerned voice brought her back.

'Oh yes of course, please ask Mr Walker to wait five minutes, then send him through.' She jumped off the bed and raced to the shower, lathering her body while she hummed to herself. Then she upended her rucksack. She picked up the Glock and weighed it in her hand. *Should she trust this stranger who had tracked her so easily?* She shrugged, pulled out her emergency dress, and pushed the gun into the bottom of the rucksack. The summer shift of soft peach coloured material and spaghetti straps was nothing fancy, but better than bike leathers and smelly t-shirts. She slipped into it, spraying herself and the room with deodorant, before kicking the rucksack into the cupboard.

Her reflection in the mirror caught her attention.

'Oh damn,' she muttered, and ran to the bathroom to brush her dark, knotted curls as much as she dared before covering her bruised head with a scarf. She thanked God she hadn't worn a disguise on the road today.

A firm rap on the door made her jump. Just her luck to want a guy who sounded like a cop about to bust the door in! She gave her hair one last tousle, poking her tongue at her make-up free face.

Sam's eyes widened when she opened the door. 'Wow, you look gorgeous, Amanda.' He reached out, touching a damp curl on her forehead. 'And to think five minutes ago, you were fast asleep.'

She frowned. 'How can you be so sure?'

'Well, I'm not a betting man, but you had more than your fair share of trouble in the desert today. Add in the fact that you also had a long ride, and it took so long for you to answer the phone, I'd put money on the possibility that you were fast asleep when reception called.'

Something about Sam's razor-sharp ability to observe and deduce caused another tingle of alarm in Mallory's subconscious. It was gone before it registered, her attention already taken by his presence in the room.

He placed a basket on the table. 'I got to thinking, and I wanted to make sure you were alright. You had an awful experience today. I figured dinner probably wasn't top on your list of priorities.'

He turned, opening the basket with a flourish. 'So, I present for your approval, a bottle of Coober Pedy's finest, two plastic cups, fresh antipasto, cheeses and crusty bread.' He put the bowls and wine on the table and looked into her eyes. 'You okay, really?'

She folded her arms. 'I guess, but I wasn't expecting company that's for sure.'

'All the same, I reckon you're hungry, right?'

She nodded, lost in his gorgeous, green eyes. He was right, but she wasn't sure exactly what she was hungry for.

He opened the bottle of wine, the dark skin on his arms smooth and sculpted in the low light of the room. She wanted to feel the strength of those arms around her, wanted him looking into her soul when he kissed her again.

He passed a cup, his fingers brushing hers. She felt her pulse jump at his touch.

He stepped toward her, and her breath caught for a moment. He raised his cup. 'To serendipity.'

Her breathing came fast and shallow as she touched her cup to his. He stared at her for a long moment and she wondered if her attraction for him was as obvious as it felt.

She cleared her throat. 'But this is no lucky coincidence. This is arranged.'

'Aren't the best ones always?' he asked.

'How did you find me?'

'I have my sources,' he laughed. 'I went to every hotel in town asking for the beautiful girl with violet eyes, until I found the right one.'

Mallory kept her face still to hide her alarm. She knew the staff had not seen her without her disguise.

He took a sip from the cup, watching her intently. 'Seriously, I had your full name, it wasn't hard to find you.'

Relief flooded through her, and she asked, 'But why?' She knew she sounded like a petulant child, but the question was out there now. She wanted it answered.

'I wanted to apologise. I shouldn't have let you go like that.' He ran a hand through his hair. 'And I wanted to see you again.'

The words sent a delicious shiver through her. She had to touch him, to feel the warmth of his body against her.

She reached out, placing her palm on his chest. He looked at her, his eyes fathomless, and took her in his arms, kissing her slowly at first, then with more insistence. She wrapped her arms around him, pressing against the length of him. He stopped and looked at her, his eyes questioning. She smiled and kissed him again. They stayed locked together for what seemed like forever, but Mallory still felt it was over too quickly when he stopped kissing her. She leant back in his arms and saw her desire mirrored in his eyes.

He smiled. 'Are we being crazy?' he asked.

'Totally. But in a good way.' She replied.

She traced a finger along the muscles on his chest.

'Who are you, Sam?'

He shrugged. 'What you see is what you get.'

'Uh uh, not so easy. Tell me more.'

'Well, what do you want to know?'

'Something. What's something you want me to know about you?'

'Well... I grew up on a station in the Northern Territory. My father was born around here but he moved to Darwin and worked as a diver on a pearler. That's where he met my mother. She was travelling. Australia was her last stop before returning to Wales.'

Mallory ran her hand down his torso as he spoke, felt the muscles contract under her touch. He grabbed her wandering hand and kissed it.

'Anyway, after they met on the pearler, they couldn't bear to be apart. They married, and took work on the station where I was born. They lived there until I finished school. Then Mum wanted to go home.'

'Wow, they must have really believed in love at first sight.'

He looked at her without speaking, his expression unreadable.

She felt a flicker of uncertainty. Did he think she was laughing at his parents. She couldn't help it that she found the idea of love at first sight ridiculous. She changed the subject. 'Are they still in Wales?'

An expression that Mallory was unable to read, again flickered across Sam's face. 'Mum went back to her family and stayed. Dad came back. He couldn't stand being away from the country he grew up in. He camps near the

Breakaways now.' He let go of her hand. 'I guess that was on my mind when you left this afternoon.'

Mallory interrupted, not wanting to investigate his line of thought. 'Is that why you're in Coober Pedy? To see your father?'

'Yep, that's it.'

The change in his voice was minute, but she noticed it. He'd closed down. She was digging too deep, too quickly. She cursed her hyper-alert reading of other people. It was making her paranoid.

She pushed away from him. 'I'm famished. How about you?'

He stepped toward her, grabbing her waist. 'I'm pretty hungry, but I've got time for one more kiss.'

She laughed as he pulled her toward him, giving in to the sensation of his lips against hers.

When he stopped, he held her face between his hands. 'You are so beautiful, Amanda Anderson.'

The sound of her alias jolted her back to reality. She had no right to question his motives. She hadn't even told this man her name, and she would have to get him out of her room before dawn or the job tomorrow would be well and truly compromised.

She pushed him away. 'We better eat before I get distracted by you, again.'

They sat cross-legged on the end of the bed and shared stories and dreams as they ate. Mallory found his tales of life on the station fascinating. Learning to read and write from a radio, living with one group of people all of his childhood, discovering how to cope with major decisions that could cost a life, enjoying a freedom most adults couldn't imagine – all of it seemed like something out of a boy's own handbook. When it was her turn, she discovered that her life in the Canadian Rockies was every bit as exotic to Sam. He couldn't picture thick snows, long, isolated winters, and nights spent drinking hot chocolate and roasting marshmallows around a fire.

Even though she knew she should make him leave, she wanted him to stay. She kept filling his cup, regaling him with stories of hikes in the mountains and holidays with her father, in the hope he would stay. In the early hours of the morning he pulled her onto his lap, kissing her neck and shoulders. She ran her hands over his face and returned his kisses, but she also knew it was time to say goodbye. She buried her face in his neck, breathing his scent of desert and wildflowers.

He kissed her one last time. 'Are you in Coober Pedy tomorrow night?'

'Yes.'

He smiled. 'Good. I want to take you out for dinner. We can talk without distractions, yeah?'

Mallory nodded, pressing down on the guilt her lie caused. By this time tomorrow night, she would be miles away from Coober Pedy, on a plane to Europe.

5

THE Underground Gallery transformed after the arrival of the Virgin Rainbow. A table was installed to take tickets, and two uniformed guards stood at attention either side of the door, while another sat beside the case in which the glowing opal was housed.

The guide Mallory saw the day before stood on the other side of the gem, expounding into a microphone. 'The Virgin Rainbow is millions of years old, and made of silica and water. It was discovered in 2003 in Coober Pedy. At only six centimetres in length, it's an extraordinary opal that looks like it is on fire on the inside, and it glows in the dark.'

The guide rattled the paper in her hand, sending ear-cracking static through the chamber. 'Experts believe the Virgin Rainbow was formed from a pocket, left by the bone of a long extinct squid with an internal skeleton, which lived in this area when it was covered by an inland sea. So, if you think there is something fishy about the Virgin Rainbow, you might be right.' She gave a bark of laughter and the speaker emitted a short burst of feedback, causing the crowd to contract toward the opposite wall.

She jumped and blurted, 'shit' into the microphone.

Titters rippled across the capacity crowd. The guide dropped the microphone, and scurried off the stage. Mallory hoped the woman would do something about the air-conditioning while she fixed the speakers. The smell of stale, sweating bodies pervaded the corridors and grottos. Wave after wave of tourists poured down the steps to stare at the fiery gem, and gasp in collective wonder when the gallery staff turned off the lights at set intervals, to allow viewings of the Virgin glowing in the dark. Every nook and cranny seemed to be packed, including the shop, where busy assistants sold cheap, pulsing replicas of the gem.

At 10.30am on the third nocturnal viewing, a shriek rang out in the gallery, followed by scuffling and shouts. The staff tried to reinstate the lights, but they wouldn't go on. Overheated patrons panicked, moving in a great swell around the main underground chamber, and becoming more and more disorientated as they jostled one another.

Mallory slipped on her night goggles and stepped behind the seated guard. He hadn't moved since the commotion started, but then she knew he wouldn't. He could tell the gem was safe – it was glowing in the darkness beside him. She looked at her watch and waited: five, four, three, two, one, bingo. The alarms were down. She leant forward, pressing her gloved hand into the back of the guard's neck, breaking his skin with the tiny serrations on the fingers. He stiffened for a moment, then his head slumped onto his chest.

She worked fast. The guard would regain consciousness in less than five minutes, with no ill effect. She tried to lift the glass off the case on the off-chance that it would be that easy. It was locked down. She dropped onto her haunches to look at the underside. Smooth, with no way in. She pulled out a glass cutter, slicing a square as closely as possible to the edges of one side of the case. She pushed the glass in and removed the

Virgin Rainbow, replacing it with a replica from the souvenir shop. Then she attached a small suction to the glass piece, pulling it back into its place, so that the cut was barely visible. She rolled the Virgin into a soft leather pouch, and pushed it deep into an inside trouser pocket. The guard started to stir as she stepped away from the case and made her way through the crowd. She'd get to the door before he realised the gem wasn't right.

Derek chattered in her ear, making her jump. *It was okay for him to yell directions, he wasn't stuck underground with a crowd of half-crazed, smelly tourists who were well on their way to panic.* She wanted to yell at him that she couldn't exactly talk to him right now, but that would have meant talking!

She moved toward the steps, the threat of a claustrophobic attack rolling over her. Stay calm, she repeated to herself, almost managing it until she saw Jimmy the Cat coming toward her. He wore night visions too, and scanned the room with a precision that chilled her. He knew someone else had the drop on the job. Images from the nightmare flooded over her, almost overpowering her ability to focus. She ducked her head and turned away, slipping her hand inside her shirt as she did to reassure herself that the Glock was still there.

She stayed low in the crowd, tracking his movements. He went straight for the guard who was standing now, staring at the false Virgin while he fumbled with his walkie-talkie. Mallory knew time was running out. Now, she had the added worry of Jimmy to deal with. He grabbed the guard, and held him close, before sitting the man in his chair. She saw a dark stain spreading across the guard's shirt when Jimmy stepped away. She put a hand over her mouth to stop the scream rising in her throat. When he discovered the jewel was gone, all hell was going to break loose.

She broke silence. 'Derek, we have company. He's just finished the guard.'

'What was the guard doing?'

'Come on, it's Jimmy the Cat. He doesn't need a reason.'

'Jesus Mal, get out of there now. I'll have the bike ready.'

She threaded toward the entrance, keeping the Cat in her sights as she went.

Jimmy bent over the case, staring at the glowing folly inside. He hung for a second before exploding, smashing his fist into the top of the case. Patrons scattered away from the noise, screaming and slamming into each other. He turned toward the entrance, staring into the milling bodies with deadly purpose.

Mallory heard him cursing behind her, and increased her pace. Her breath came in sharp gasps. She needed to slow down, remain aware, and above all, stay calm. The crowd swelled around her, their movements wild and erratic. She let herself be carried toward the steps by a wave of bodies, was almost there; would be on her way to safety when she reached them. She jumped onto the bottom step, and started to leap her way to freedom when her left arm jerked backwards with such force, it left her socket burning.

There was no point using her body weight against Jimmy. He would stab her as soon as she came close. She ignored the pain and swung on the full arc of her arm, bringing her legs up as she did, kicking him with both feet in the stomach. He grunted and dropped, still holding her arm in an iron fist. The crowd jostled around the two thieves, panicking as the thump of feet on flesh transmitted through their bodies. Mallory realised a stampede was imminent, and bit into his hand. He screamed and let go. She leapt up the steps, three at a time, and turned for one last look behind, fearful he would come after her, grab her by the hair, and plunge a knife into her back. She stopped at the sight of Sam pushing his way through the crowd toward the fallen guard. She shook her head, pulled off the night goggles, and slipped through the door.

On the floor below, Jimmy saw her face as she turned and hesitated at the door. 'Got you, young Cash,' he whispered. He curled into a ball, and rolled toward the bottom of the steps.

***

Every nerve screamed in Mallory's body as Derek idled along the main drag out of town. She wanted to yell at him to get the hell out, but he was doing the right thing. Taking his time, pointing at shops and hotels like a tourist. After all, there was a good chance the authorities hadn't been alerted. Why draw attention? When they reached the area where the mullock heaps started, he left the highway and zigzagged through the mounds of debris until the road was no longer visible. Mallory dismounted, her body shaking with adrenalin. She peeled off a layer of black clothes, packing her gun and supplies into the camouflage pants she wore beneath.

'Where's the Virgin?' Derek asked.

She pulled out the leather roll and revealed the opal.

'It doesn't look like much to me.'

'It glows in the dark.'

'So do Lightning Bugs.'

Mallory stroked the opal. 'There's something about it, though. It's got a fire to it. I think it's pretty damn special.' She rolled it into the leather and pushed the pouch back into the inner button-down pocket in her trousers. 'Let's get those dirt bikes, and get out of here.'

The pair pulled a sandy coloured tarpaulin off an old mine entrance, and jogged into the derelict shaft. They took the wrong path, turned back on themselves twice, and spent a moment laughing and high-fiving in relief when they found the bikes, exactly where Trafford said they would be.

Derek said, 'Christ Mal, this job is like taking candy from babies.' He stared at the bikes, rubbing his chin. 'Hey, why don't we just take one bike and travel light? We're on the home run.'

'No, that's a bad idea. We need a backup; in case something happens to one of them.' She gunned her ride before he could argue, and weaved through the mullock heaps.

'You got your coordinates locked in?'

Derek's voice in her earpiece made her jump, causing the bike to skitter sideways. 'Yes, on track for William Creek near Lake Eyre.'

'The Woomera area is prohibited. Stay on the track. We don't need the bloody armed forces on our tail. By the end of the day, we'll be on a chopper out of this Godforsaken hole. And don't get too far ahead. I want you where I can see you.'

She raised a thumb in his direction, hoping he would shut up. The image of Sam pushing his way toward the guard returned as she rode through the mullock heaps. She felt her heart give a painful lurch. She wondered why he was at the gallery, but pushed thoughts of him away. She didn't need the distraction at a time like this.

They stopped after forty minutes to rest and rehydrate. The terrain was unforgiving, the heat suffocating, making it hard to stay focused and ride.

When they remounted, Derek said, 'You should give me the Virgin for safe keeping.'

Mallory stared at him, her gaze unflinching. 'No, not after last time.'

'That was different. Come on, we have to work together.'

'Yes, that's true. But we don't have to trust each other.'

After she started her bike, she turned off the earpiece so she wouldn't have to listen to Derek trying to scam her, and left him in a pall of dust. The bike handled like a dream, jumping ruts and hummocks with ease. It was liberating, playing in the desert on a real dirt bike. She forgot about Derek. The ride brought back a rush of holiday memories from all of the times she'd spent in Turkey with her parents. Having grown up in Canada, the arid Turkish landscape fascinated her. Her dad took her riding every day, teaching her how to jump the bike and do skiddies on terrain that was so different to their home in the Rockies, while her mum visited markets and haggled with vendors. Mallory hadn't known that her father was a jewel thief then; had been too young to think of him as anything but her dad.

The sound of a powerful motor to the left brought her back to the present. She glanced over her shoulder and saw Jimmy the Cat bearing down on her in a sand buggy. She cursed, darted to the right and braked, pulling the bike around in the opposite direction. She scanned the track for Derek, but there was no sign of him. She gunned the bike and zipped into the dunes beside the track.

Jimmy brought the buggy around and gave chase. When he came up beside her again, he held a crossbow in one hand, and aimed at her. She hung the bike sideways, grabbing her Glock as she did, pumping a round at the bow. The weapon flew into the air. She caught a glimpse of Jimmy's contorted face before the buggy disappeared behind her. She crossed the track and rode toward Coober Pedy, keeping to the smaller dunes, but there was no sign of Derek.

She stopped for a moment and turned on her earpiece. 'Derek? Where are you?'

'Jesus! Fuck! Where have you been? I thought the Cat had your tongue. I tried to stop him, but he got away from me. It was like he knew I didn't have the opal.'

'I bet he saw me at the gallery.'

'Shit, shit, shit!'

'Don't worry, he found me already. I lost him,' she said.

'Thank Christ. Keep heading toward Lake Eyre. Don't worry, I'm on my way.'

Mallory turned the bike around and saw Jimmy at the top of a dune, a rifle trained on her.

'Oh hell, Derek. He's got me. I'm on the right side of the track,' she whispered.

'Keep your earpiece on. I'll find you.'

She put both hands up, waiting for Jimmy to approach. He revved the buggy and drove toward her, the rifle still aimed at her chest.

When he drew close he yelled, 'Hello, young Cash. You're not half the man your father was.'

'What would you know?'

'More than you.' He stepped out of the vehicle. 'Now don't worry, I'm not going to kill you. Not yet.'

Her heart lurched. He was a cruel son of a bitch.

'Where's my Rainbow?'

She shrugged. 'Somewhere over.'

'Don't try to be clever, Cash, you're not good at it. We can trade. Don't you want to know where your father is?'

Mallory's heart contracted. 'You *are* an asshole, Cat.'

'Be polite. Don't you want to know where your old man is hiding?'

Her arms trembled. She concentrated on holding them still.

'Tempting isn't it, young Cash, to find your old man again. To discover what he thinks of his daughter following in his footsteps. Do you think he would be proud of you?'

'Shut up. You shouldn't talk about him.'

'Why not? Me and Warwick, we go way back.'

The sound of her father's first name hit her hard. Nobody but family used his first name.

'That's right. I know your daddy's first name. One of the select, eh? We were tight War and me, once upon a time.'

'Bullshit.' She couldn't reconcile the father she knew

with the picture the Cat was painting. Her dad was always saving lame ducks, helping people in need. He was a good man who supported his family with money made on the wrong side of the law, but he was no killer. There was no way he would hang with Jimmy.

She shook her head.

'Now don't tell me you don't want to know. That's the wrong answer.'

'This isn't your style, Cat. Why do you want the opal so bad?'

He laughed. 'Alright, let's talk about the Virgin. My client's an angry man who wants to make enemy nations pay.' Jimmy shrugged. 'He's going to crush that opal. I don't know why. I don't care as long as I get my money. It's a piece of old rock that isn't worth much.'

Mallory felt the warmth of the opal through the leather pouch in her pocket, and resisted the urge to cover it with a protective hand. She shifted on the bike, ready to defend the gem.

The faint vibration of a motorbike engine broke the silence. Jimmy lifted his head, sniffing the air like an animal. 'Your man, Derek, is coming to save the day.' He lifted the rifle, pulled back the bolt, and stared down the sight at Mallory.

'I don't have the Virgin Rainbow.'

'Give it.' His finger curled around the trigger.

The world slowed down, as though a movie were playing and she the only watcher. She shook her head from side to side, trying to process what was happening. *She was going to die in this desert today.*

Derek's bike sounded as though it were still a long way off, but he appeared out of nowhere, jumping a dune behind Jimmy and slamming into his back. Jimmy threw his arms up as he fell and the rifle discharged. Derek and the bike fell out of the air, and time righted itself as Mallory ran to her fallen partner to help him to his feet.

Derek's eyes were wild as he threw a fist in the air.

'Bullseye, Mal!'

The sound of an approaching vehicle made them hang onto each other for a moment. 'Army?' he mouthed, before they stumbled toward her undamaged bike.

He jumped on behind her, looking at his watch as they sped away. He wrapped his arms around her and yelled, 'We've got to hurry. The chopper will leave if we don't make the time.'

Mallory struggled to keep the bike straight in the deep ruts along the track. Her arms and back strained, fatigued. Derek slumped against her. She had no way of knowing whether he was injured or sleeping. She wondered if she should stop and check on him when the bike sputtered, and the engine cut out.

Derek sat up. 'What's up?'

'We're out of fuel.'

'Shit. There was a can on the other bike. I forgot it.'

They looked at each other without speaking. Jimmy would come after them. It was possible the army was in the area. If they waited on the road, they would get a group hug from hell. They pulled the water bottles off the bike, took the key, and started to walk.

We could go into the dunes where it's easier to hide,' Derek suggested.

'We wouldn't make it. Too hard going. Too hot.'

Neither of them voiced their uppermost thoughts. They had no chance of making the meeting point now. They would be lucky to make it out of the desert alive.

***

Mallory's lips were cracking, and her tongue felt swollen and dry. She glanced at Derek. He staggered when his boot caught in a rut. She put one foot in front of the other, pushing her body to do as she commanded.

'What's that?' Derek pointed at an indistinct shape in the heat ahead.

'Mirage,' she whispered.

The mirage continued toward them, solidifying into a strange alliance of man, camel and machine.

When the contraption drew closer, Derek let out a dry chuckle. 'Only in Australia, Mal.'

She stopped and stared at the beaten up single-cab ute, of an indiscriminate type and colour, being towed by six camels. There was no roof on the vehicle, and the motor was not running. A man sat in the driver's seat, steering the camels over the bonnet. He waved a dirty hand toward them, his full smile visible beneath the brim of his hat. Another man, wearing a sweat-stained Akubra and mirrored sunglasses, slumped in the passenger seat. He did not acknowledge their presence.

The vehicle drew level, and the driver pulled the animals to a halt.

'G'day. You come here often?' he asked, letting out huge bellows of laughter at his own wit, slapping his leg and kicking a boot against the floor of the ute. His bulbous nose had the glow of too much sun and alcohol. When he pushed his hat back and smiled, he revealed a line of snowy white skin above his terracotta face, pale blue eyes and large, uneven teeth. His companion sat up. Despite the mirrored sunglasses, Mallory felt him staring at her.

She reached for her Glock. After her encounter with the tattooed man the day before, she was in no mood to take chances with an eccentric stranger.

Derek put a calming hand on her forearm. 'Our bike broke down on the track. We need to get to Lake Eyre.'

The man broke into fresh gales of laughter. 'Well you're in a spot of bother, aren't you, old chap,' he replied, mimicking Derek's plummy English accent.

Mallory considered shooting the annoying old bastard and taking his transport. Her fingers closed around her gun, her thumb itching to cock the hammer. Derek gave her a warning look. She let go of the Glock and concentrated on breathing slowly.

'Can you help us?' Derek asked, with infinite patience.

'Depends on what you mean by help,' the man said.

'Can we buy your ute?'

'Nuh.' He looked them up and down. 'You seem alright. I might sell you a camel or two, depending on what you have to offer.'

Mallory wanted to tell him to go away so she could die in peace, but of course, that wasn't how it would be. She watched Derek weighing up the idea. He would strike a deal, because even when he was half dead, he was a natural wheeler-dealer.

The man in the passenger seat sat up and nudged his companion. 'The Virgin is here.'

'Hey enough of that,' said the driver, pushing the older man away. 'Sorry mate, we're not like that,' he said to Mallory. 'The old fella's blind. He doesn't know what he's saying.'

The man in the mirrored sunglasses pushed the driver's hand away impatiently, and pointed at her. 'She has the Virgin fire. Ask her!'

'We have the key to a good Yamaha dirt bike,' Derek interrupted. 'The bike is about six miles back on the track, that way.' He pointed toward Coober Pedy.

The driver frowned at his muttering passenger. 'Shut up old man.' He looked at Derek, all traces of humour gone. 'Not interested in a maybe bike. Sure, I'll take the key, but I need something else.'

Derek folded his arms, pushing his boot back and forth through the sand, as though he had other options to consider.

Mallory sighed. Whether she liked it or not ,she was going to have to ride out of this mess on a bloody camel!

'We don't have time for this crap,' she said. She pulled out her wallet. 'Three hundred. Take it or leave it.'

The driver tied the reins to the steering wheel, and jumped out of the vehicle. 'That's more like it.' He looked at Derek. 'And what about you, mate?'

Derek shook his head. The man shrugged. 'These camels are worth their weight in gold. Don't go thinking I'm giving them away.'

Derek pulled out his wallet, and handed over the last of his money.

The man sniffed the notes, added them to Mallory's, and flicked each one as he counted. 'Thousand will do nice,' he said.

'What about water?' Derek asked.

The man laughed as he unhitched the camels. 'No one will sell you water out here.' He turned to his companion. 'Talk about mad dogs and Englishmen, eh Bob?'

Bob tracked Mallory's movements without answering. She shivered.

The driver led the camels to Derek, passing him the lead lines. 'Now, watch and learn.' He turned to the camels, holding up a hand. 'Tuk, Tuk.'

They groaned and dropped onto the ground, folding their legs beneath them. 'Get on then, quick sticks,' the man said.

The pair climbed onto the beasts, clinging to the flimsy saddles on their backs.

'Hoi, Hoi,' commanded the man.

The camels stood. Mallory bit down on a scream. Vivid memories of her last ride returned; the feeling of losing control, of being stuck on an ungainly creature who could run like the wind. The camel snorted, looking around at her with a knowing eye. She relaxed, aware her nerves could spook the animal, and put her in real danger.

'Now when you want them to move forward or stop, it's just like riding a horse. Click when you want to go and say whoa when you want to stop. Don't bother about those lead lines – they're only there to make you feel like you're in control.' He broke into bellowing laughter again, as if his last statement was the funniest thing imaginable.

'Is that all?' Derek asked.

The man stopped laughing. 'Wait, just had a thought.'

He went back to the ute, and dragged two rolls of pale material out of a bag. He threw one up to each rider. 'Wrap yourselves in these, or you'll fry up there.'

Mallory grabbed the cloth. It was surprisingly clean and soft. She wrapped it around her body and head and felt immediately cooler. She smiled at the man.

He smiled back. 'You're welcome, sweetheart.'

Mallory and Derek looked at each other. He raised his eyes, and she nodded. They started down the track in stately slow motion.

As if reading their thoughts, the man yelled, 'Don't worry about the pace. They cover more ground than you think.' He trotted between them, handing a switch to each rider. 'Just in case you get in a spot, and need some speed. But be careful about asking them to run. They're used to racing.'

Bob stood up as they passed the ute and yelled, 'Don't let them go! Don't take the Virgin away!'

'Jesus wept Bob, what's got into you? Would you stop talking about friggin' virgins, already!'

Mallory looked back at the old man in the mirrored sunglasses. He pointed a finger at her. 'Hold onto the Rainbow, and you will die.'

She clicked at the camel, wanting to put miles between her and the blind man with supernatural sight as quickly as possible.

***

The riders slowly adjusted to the rock and roll of the camel's gait, and the miles passed at a sedate pace. Mallory felt the frustration coming off Derek. He was stressing about the time they were losing, but she was more or less resigned to the turn of events. She watched the landscape drifting by, trying to see it in the way Sam had shown her. It still appeared desolate and uninhabitable for the most part, but every so often the veil lifted, and she caught a glimpse of the secret life of the desert at the edge of her vision.

The sound of an approaching vehicle put the riders on red alert. She clicked the camel, closing the gap between herself and Derek. 'Should we leave the road?'

'Not sure we can. Do you know how to steer these things?'

'We have to figure it out. Let's assume it's like riding a horse. If we want them to go left, we should look left and move our weight in that direction.'

They tried her suggestion, and after what seemed an eternity the camels began to leave the track.

The sound of the motor grew louder, the noise grating in the silence. 'We need to get into those smallish drifts over there,' Derek said urgently, pointing further off the road. He started to click and kick at the same time. His camel lifted into the air as it broke into a canter, making him yell with delight, but Mallory felt no joy when her camel followed suit. The rocking motion was gone, replaced by a rough, bone-shaking gait that threatened to tip her off. She clung to the saddle, clenching her teeth to avoid screaming as the dunes approached with surprising speed. She drew level with Derek. He grinned at her with enjoyment.

'How do we stop them?' she gasped.

'Don't know. Just keep them pointed in the right direction until they run out of puff.' He smiled as though finally satisfied they were getting somewhere.

The sound of the motor faded away. Mallory knew they couldn't run forever, but the animals seemed to be bent on trying. It took all of her concentration to hold her nerve while they cantered up and down dunes, and snorted to each other. When they finally slowed to a loping walk, she thought she would fall off from exhaustion. She grabbed her water bottle, drinking until it emptied. Her mount turned and looked at her, as if judging her stupidity in their current situation.

She looked into its face and poked her tongue.
'Shut up, you.'

The camel shook its head, and huffed.

They walked with the sun at their backs now, the desert already cooling as the afternoon started to draw in.

Derek checked his watch. 'We've got a three-hour window before they leave. We have to get going.'

They clicked the camels into a canter, and let the animals set their own pace. As they made their way back onto the track near William Creek, Derek's camel startled and jumped over a snake on the side of the road, upending him in the process. He rolled as he hit the rutted surface, coming back onto his feet with surprising speed. The snake lifted off the ground, ready to strike at any target in the confusion.

Mallory realised the camel would run off, and hers would follow. She pushed closer to Derek's camel and grabbed the flying lead line, relieved when the panicked animal listened to the tug on the rope.

Derek yelled. She turned in time to see him dancing across the road, with the angry snake in hot pursuit. As he bolted toward the camels, the cloth he wore unravelled behind him like a giant sail. His eyes were wide and white in his dirty face, his hair standing on end from the dust and heat. He was a far cry from the smooth, groomed Englishman who met her in the bar two days ago. She laughed as he vaulted up the side of his camel.

He looked over at her. 'What's so bloody funny?'

'You,' she said, and laughed harder.

He frowned. 'Glad it amuses you.' He clicked at the camel to go.

Tears streamed down her face, and her sides hurt as she followed him, but she couldn't stop laughing. This job was by far the strangest one she had ever had the misfortune to accept.

6

LIGHT aircraft sat idle on the overheated tarmac of the small aerodrome at William Creek. Mallory looked at them, imagining a different trip to the one she had just endured. They could have hired a plane, hopping over here from Coober Pedy. They would have had time for lunch and a cold beer, probably even an afternoon nap before they left. Of course, she knew her daydream was impossible. Their trail would have been easy to follow. All the same, the feeling that she'd been duped by circumstances persisted.

A few locals hung under the shade of the verandah around the pub. They lifted their beers in silence, as though the sight of strangers appearing out of the desert on camels was an everyday occurrence in the town. The pair pushed onwards to the meeting point, midway between William Creek and Marree, on the shore of Lake Eyre. The lake stretched over the horizon, sometimes looking like a giant mirrored sky, others like nothing more than a dried-up salt pan. By the time they reached their destination, Mallory was sick of the heat and the thirst, and the pain in her butt caused from riding a camel for hours over rough terrain.

Stealing the Virgin Rainbow had seemed simple in the beginning, but it had turned into a nightmare when Jimmy the Cat got involved. His offer to tell her where her father was located, and the memory of him pointing the rifle at her head, haunted her. If she said yes, and gave him the Virgin, would she know where her father was now? No, it would be worse than stupid to contemplate the idea that Jimmy would keep his word. If she had agreed, she would be dead now, and he would have the Virgin. There was also the mystery of the other vehicle. She'd read that it was possible to go for weeks without seeing another traveller on that particular track. Perhaps it was an army vehicle after all, but what were the chances of someone coming so close to them, in such an isolated area?

At last, the thumping whoomp of an approaching chopper broke the silence. Mallory unwound the cloth swathing her and let it drift to the ground. The pair brought the camels together. The trials they'd been through sluiced away old grievances, forging a newfound bond between them. They touched each other's hands in a gentle high-five, and flicked their sticks on the rumps of the animals. The camels broke into a rough gallop, heading straight onto the lake. The helicopter appeared like a magical bird out of the dusty haze, and Derek let out a jubilant whoop.

The chopper descended, whipping their hair and clothes, and covering them in salt spray. The camels bellowed in fear as they ran into the heart of the lake, until the couple steered them around, bringing them back under the low-hanging chopper. As soon as he drew close enough, Derek stood in the saddle and grabbed a skid, swinging onto it with the ease of a circus performer. He sat, and held out a hand to Mallory.

She gripped the saddle, shaking her head. There was no way she was standing up on one of these stupid animals! He signalled to the watching pilot. The chopper dropped another notch. She grinned as she reached up to him. *Such a gentleman when she was holding the bounty!* She grabbed his hand, and he flipped her up onto the platform. She turned and helped him up, then sat for a moment to catch her breath, before turning to thank him.

Derek was staring across the lake toward the car park. The expression on his face startled her. She followed his gaze. A white 4WD sped towards them across the dry bed of the lake. Derek swore, pulling out his binoculars.

She stood up and shaded her eyes. 'Is it Jimmy?'

He shook his head. 'Never seen this one before.'

He passed the glasses to her. She readjusted the focus and saw a flashing light on the roof of the vehicle. She moved the binoculars to the driver. Sam's face filled the lens. She gasped, and steadied herself on the cabin wall.

'Do you know him?'

She couldn't speak. The vehicle drew closer. Sam's face was visible without the aid of binoculars now. She knew he would be able to see her, too. She wanted to hide from him, but there was nowhere to go. Something heavy thumped into the helicopter behind her, making it shudder for a moment, but her thoughts were too taken with Sam to register the noise.

Derek watched the blood draining from her face. 'Shit Mallory. What have you done?'

She realised Sam hadn't told her what he did for a

living. She was so into him it wasn't a question she considered asking. It all made sense now. The way he helped her when she was hurt, his tracking abilities and keen observation. Why hadn't he told her he was a cop after she was attacked? She cursed her own blindness, and marvelled at his. *He must have been working undercover to ensure the Virgin didn't get stolen. She'd been under his nose the entire time!*

The hairs on the back of her neck prickled. She turned in time to see Jimmy the Cat crossing the cabin. He landed on Derek's back before she could yell a warning. The two men rolled around the floor with limbs flying. The thump of fists on flesh and boots on metal echoed throughout the aircraft. Mallory pulled out the Glock, but thought better of it. A warning shot might hit the wrong thing, or ricochet, and send the chopper tumbling. She put the Glock away, and tried to grab hold of Jimmy, but she couldn't tell who was who.

Suddenly the pair stopped moving. Jimmy rose with a dripping knife in his hand. Derek lay where he left him, a pool of blood spreading beneath his body.

'Give me the Virgin Rainbow,' Jimmy panted.

She shook her head, reaching for the Glock. He stepped to the side of the platform and looked at the 4WD below. 'I wouldn't do that.'

She aimed the Glock at his head.

He smiled, unperturbed. 'You were paying an awful lot of attention. Know him, do you?'

She shook her head.

'Hand it over.' He studied her face, as though he had all the time in the world to get what he wanted. She held her ground, refusing to be bluffed.

He turned away and pulled out his gun, crouching to

take aim at Sam. 'Time for some target practice, then.'

'No!'

He spoke without looking at her, his gun still on Sam. 'Put that gun away. Give me the Virgin.'

She put her gun in the holster, pulled the leather pouch out of her pants, holding it where he could see it.

His narrow face filled with mean triumph. 'I wish your old man had seen that. He'd be shamed.'

Heat flushed through her at his words. She looked down at Sam. He was talking into a radio, his gun trained on the chopper. She wondered if he would shoot her. The aircraft was hovering above him, while the pilot waited for instructions.

She watched him watching her, felt his eyes lock with hers. She knew her disguise was not one of her best, and wondered if he recognised her.

'I'm sorry,' she whispered. She remembered what the old man in the desert had said. She would die if she tried to take the Virgin with her. *She had to get the opal off this helicopter.* She glanced at the vehicle below, and knew what she had to do. Oblivious to anyone but Sam, she flung back her arm, intent on throwing the gem to the waiting policeman below.

Before she had time to complete the throw, Jimmy the Cat stepped toward her, and slammed his gun into the side of her head.

7

THE Superintendent drummed his fingers on the desk. 'Are you sure there wasn't a woman with Jimmy Contanti and Derek James, Walker?'

Sam shook his head. 'I'm certain, sir.'

'Strange. Contanti insists he was working alone, but I know Eve Saldino was in the mix somewhere. As you know, one of her goons was picked up near Alice Springs. But we can't find any intelligence linking her to this operation, or even placing her in Australia at the time.' The older man flicked through the pages of the report, before nodding at his notes. 'But I feel certain she's involved. Shame Derek James didn't survive – I think we can take Contanti's word on that – no love lost there.' He sighed. 'We could have done with James' version of events. I'm surprised the bastards on the chopper didn't throw him out the door.'

'Perhaps there's honour amongst thieves after all?'

The Super snorted. 'Doubt it. The fact that there was no body still gives me some pause for thought on Jimmy Contanti's story. What do you think Detective Inspector?'

He looked up, his mild, quizzical expression not fooling Sam for a moment.

Sam shrugged. 'Afraid I can't answer that, sir.'

'Did you see the body, Walker?'

'No. Unfortunately the local contingent was all over everything when I got there. Nobody seemed to know what was going on.'

The Super sighed. 'Well, we have the notorious cat in a cage, but no Virgin Rainbow, a possible femme fatale who's gone AWOL, and a missing dead man.' He banged the report on his desk, aligning the edges with obsessive precision before placing it into the folder. 'There's too many loose ends. I'm not happy, Walker.'

Sam stood up. 'I'm sorry, sir.'

The Super studied him. 'You know Walker, I reckon you're overdue for a break.'

His words found their mark. Sam knew better than to argue. 'Actually sir, I was thinking of heading out to see my father.'

'Yes. I reckon that might be a good idea. Get out of here for a while.'

Sam returned to his desk. He knew he didn't have much time to get the information he needed. He opened a file on his computer, searching through columns of female faces until they started to blur into one. He clicked past a woman who appeared more like a favourite aunt than a criminal, then paused. The disguise was amazing, but he recognised something in the wary expression. The sight of her among some of the most dangerous women in the world shook him. He scribbled the name on a piece of paper. At least it was somewhere to start. He looked toward the Superintendent's office, wondering once again if he were doing the right thing. After all, he didn't know why exactly, but he was certain she had intended to throw the opal to him. Instinct told him she was no killer, either. He couldn't believe she was responsible for the guard at the gallery. All the same, his professional integrity and training told him he should reveal her presence at Lake Eyre to the Super.

He scanned the information on her sheet, and let out a low whistle. The alias, and he was sure it would be, had form. But it was the side notes from Interpol that fascinated him. Interpol felt certain her real name was Mallory Cash, but there was no way to prove the theory. Her old man was a notorious gentleman robber; a slippery, cunning operator, hated by Interpol, and loved by the public for his Robin Hood behaviour. Sam checked Warwick Cash's record. The last time he'd been spotted was in Portugal thirteen years ago. There was no mention of any activity from him since. Was it possible he had retired, and relied on his daughter to make the money? Or had he died?

He looked around the deserted office, before tracing a finger over the lines of her face. He closed the file and rested his head in his hands. He was tired, and couldn't tell what was right and wrong when it came to her. The best thing for him to do would be to go to the Breakaways, sit with his dad and talk. They could camp, and he could sharpen his tracking skills in the bush. Perhaps he would even find a good time to ask for advice, but then, his old man could only tell him about his own experiences with a girl from another country. He opened the file and stared at her face again. *Was it really an option to hang out there in the desert for a while and forget about her?* Even as he weighed it up, he knew he couldn't do it.

He took his badge and gun, placed them on his desk, pulled open a drawer, and grabbed his passport and wallet. When he stood up, his eyes focused on a point far from where he stood. He took one last look at the woman on the screen before switching off the computer, and whispered, 'I'm coming for you, Mallory Cash.'

8

MALLORY groaned and rolled onto her side. She opened her eyes and focused on her surroundings. The garish wallpaper and mousey smell in the freezing room made her stomach lurch. She squeezed her eyes shut. The last thing she remembered was the disappointment on Sam's face as she hovered above him in the chopper, and her decision to return the Virgin to him. Her eyes snapped open. She sat up, stopping when dizziness hit her. She ran her hands over her pockets, but her gun and the Virgin were gone. *Where was she? And what had happened to the Virgin?*

Her nose twitched while she tried to sort through her jumbled memories. The mousey smell was emanating from below the bed. She looked at a chipped dresser pushed under a tiny window, and the rusted iron frame of the bed she lay upon. With the exception of the crazy wallpaper, the tiny room felt very much like a cell. Her throat closed in panic at the thought of being trapped.

She forced herself to breathe deeply, swung her legs over the edge of the bed and pressed her feet onto the bare floorboards. She shivered, grabbing a robe on the end of her bed and wrapping it around her shoulders. When she reached the heavy wooden door, she stopped for a moment to steady her breathing. Her relief at finding the door unlocked was short-lived when she saw where she was. Nuns moved silently around a high-walled courtyard outside the room. One of them stopped when she saw Mallory standing at the door.

She approached with a warm smile. 'How are you feeling today?'

Mallory frowned. 'How long have I been here?'

'Two weeks. When your sister brought you here, she said you had been through a terrible ordeal.' She placed a gentle hand on the side of Mallory's head. 'The wound you sustained on your head has healed, but we thought it best to let you alone until you came back to yourself.'

'My sister?'

'Yes, a lovely girl. There is no need to feel ashamed. She explained that you have fallen on hard times. She wanted to make sure you were safe.' The nun stepped back and surveyed Mallory. 'We continued with the medication she gave us. She said you needed to stay sedated until you healed.' The nun's eyes lit up. 'Oh, and she said to tell you that Jim sends his regards.'

Mallory's insides turned to ice. *Whoever dropped her here was working for Jimmy the Cat.*

'Where am I?' she asked.

'You are at the Carmel of St. Joseph Monastery, Armstrong.'

'Armstrong? Armstrong, Canada?' Mallory asked.

The nun nodded.

Shock made Mallory feel faint. She staggered back into the room and dropped onto the bed. *How was it possible that she could be transported halfway across the world, and not remember anything? How could she lose two weeks, even with sedation?* She dropped her head into her hands, and tried to remember what had transpired on the helicopter, but the last thing she could conjure was the look on Sam's face.

The nun followed her into the room. 'You can stay here as long as you need, dear.'

She shook her head. 'I want to go home.'

The nun nodded. 'Of course. Come to Mother Superior's office when you are ready. Your possessions are in safekeeping there.' She opened the dresser, removed Mallory's laundered clothing, and placed it on the bed beside her.

Mallory pushed her anxiety aside while she dressed. She would find out soon enough whether she still had a passport to use. Not that it really mattered. She was in her home country, and she had plenty of spares. She opened the door, jumping with fright when a different nun stepped out of the shadows. The woman smiled, but it did not reach her eyes. It was clear that she knew Mallory was not the kind of girl who belonged in a nunnery. When they reached the office, Mallory signed a sheet, and took a duffel bag she did not recognise. At the large wooden doors leading to the outside world, the nun murmured goodbye, swinging them shut with determined finality before Mallory could reply. She crouched down, and rummaged through the bag. The passport she had used to enter Australia, her wallet and her keys were there, along with a jacket she didn't recognise. She went through the pockets but found no clue to the owner. She opened her wallet. The few dollars she'd kept aside were gone, but her credit cards were still there. A piece of paper caught her eye. She pulled it out. The words, YOU ARE A DEAD GIRL WALKING written in thick, red marker, made her flush hot and cold with fear.

***

Mallory approached her home along a trail through the stands of Black Spruce that surrounded her property. The trail was rarely used, and due to the difficulty of moving through Spruce, unlikely to be discovered by strangers. She crouched, peering through a gap in the hedge surrounding the house. There were no signs of life, nothing appeared to be disturbed. She checked the small traps she had set around the perimeter. They were not designed to cause pain, but would definitely show disturbance if anyone had entered the property. When everything appeared to be in order, she approached the house, and conducted another sweep of the perimeter. Once inside, she saw no intrusions had occurred, and her body relaxed.

She slumped onto the couch and let go of the tension that had been building since she woke in the monastery yesterday. She looked out the window at The Three Sisters and felt the security of home envelop her. It was so good to be back in Canmore, surrounded by the mountains she loved. All the same, she was in serious danger. She didn't have the Virgin Rainbow, and she didn't know where it was. What's more, she didn't know where Jimmy the Cat, or Derek, were either. If Jimmy the Cat had the Virgin Rainbow, both she and Derek were as good as dead. She turned the events she could remember over and over, but the whole mess made no sense. *Why would Jimmy send her to a monastery to be nursed back to health?* No matter what angle she looked at the situation from, Jimmy's involvement in her rescue was sinister and yet, highly unlikely. She hoped Derek had somehow taken possession of the Virgin and delivered it to Trafford. He would take the glory, but at least she wouldn't be on the receiving end of Trafford's rage. She sighed and dropped her head into her hands. Visions of Sam, sitting cross-legged on the bed and talking about his childhood returned to her. She remembered his expression, so open and innocent, and felt her heart lurch. He was a cop! *Bastard!* There was no way she would ever see him again. She felt tears threatening, and pushed her fists into her sockets until her eyes hurt. She needed sleep. Then it would be time to contact Trafford and face the music.

9

'WHERE'S the Virgin?'

Mallory took a deep breath. 'Here's the thing Trafford, Jimmy the Cat was there. He brought the heat down on us when we reached the rendezvous point.'

'Do you know who he was working for?' Trafford showed no surprise at her revelation.

She wondered how he knew Jimmy was in Coober Pedy. 'Nope. You know how he likes to monologue. He said something about his client wanting to crush the Rainbow to make enemy states suffer.'

'Well speaking of that, where is my lovely Virgin Rainbow now?'

Her gut clenched. 'I don't know.'

Trafford's silence was more disturbing than his anger. When he finally spoke, he was so quiet she had to lean toward the screen to hear him. 'Jimmy the Cat is in custody. They didn't find that opal on him. Derek James is dead. He can't lie to protect you. You better tell me the truth.'

'What?'

'Surely you know?' He dived toward the camera, his

shark eyes so large in the monitor that she flinched involuntarily.

'You really don't know.' He let out a mirthless chuckle. 'Ah well, it's the world we live in, Cash. Easy come, easy go.'

She swallowed the thick lump in her throat, and willed her eyes to stay dry. She would say her goodbyes to Derek in private.

Trafford hit his desk, making her jump. 'So, the word on the street is, the Cat swallowed a canary while he was underground in Australia, and is currently singing like a bird. Do you know what he's saying?'

Mallory shrugged. 'Why should I?'

'He's telling anyone who will listen that he tangled with Eve Saldino in Australia. Now I'm sure you can appreciate that my Eve is not happy. After all, when she does a job, she does it right. And let's face it, Cash, when it comes to physical presence, you are no Eve.'

She kept her face still. It made no sense for the Cat to imply that it was not Mallory, but Eve, on the helicopter. *Unless he had plans.* A chill ran over her body. She couldn't rely on the Australian penal system to keep the Cat indoors. She was certain she hadn't seen the last of him.

'Pay attention, Cash!'

She returned her focus to the short, balding man on her screen. He was so nondescript it was almost laughable, but there were plenty of dead men who had made the mistake of underestimating his capacity for violence. For a moment she savoured the idea of giving him a thrashing, but that was not within her capabilities right now.

His eyes darkened as if he had read her mind. 'Just bring me the Virgin Rainbow.'

'Derek was holding it.'

He held up a hand. 'I'm not a monster.'

She almost snorted out loud.

Trafford adjusted the camera, the sudden light washing out his features. 'I give you the benefit of the doubt, Cash, because I had so much respect for your father, and I accept that you had the fight of your life getting out of there.' His eyes narrowed. 'The thing is, I paid for my Virgin. You don't get to change the plan because things get rough.'

He stopped speaking while he adjusted the zoom on his camera again. 'Bring it. Perhaps I will call us square.'

'I don't have it.'

'You have six weeks, or I send Eve to exact payment.' He sat back and stared at her with satisfaction. All he needed was a fluffy, white cat on his lap to complete the "villain supreme" character he was working so hard to cultivate. It would be laughable, if he weren't so dangerous.

It occurred to her that this was the first time she had spoken to him without Eve hovering in the background.

The question was out before she had time to stop herself. 'Where is Eve, anyway?'

He picked up a gun, pointing it at her until the barrel filled the screen. 'Don't try to play me, Cash. You won't live to regret it.'

The screen went black. Mallory stood up, flinging her chair into the wall. Derek was dead, and she was asking stupid questions that didn't matter when she was likely to get killed in the near future! She pressed her fists into her eyes. Her life had turned to crap overnight, and even though Derek was a narcissistic bastard, he didn't deserve to die on a chopper in the middle of nowhere. And Sam, a guy she'd felt so connected to, was a cop, who would, no doubt, love to hunt her down, after the lies she had told him. It was likely she would lose her life as well, because if the Cat didn't have the opal, she had no idea where the Virgin Rainbow could be.

Mallory decided she didn't have time to give in to anger and disillusion. She switched off the computer and started packing. There was no point hanging around, waiting for trouble to come to her. She had to find the

Virgin Rainbow, or run somewhere Trafford would never find her. She dropped to the floor, untacking a join in her bedroom carpet, and rolling it to one side to reveal a trapdoor. As she descended into the cellar, the bone numbing coldness below ground goose-bumped her arms, making her rub at them and shiver. She moved quickly to the safe and rolled and clicked through the combination. She swung the heavy door open and grabbed a gun, money and a passport.

As she turned toward the stairs, a slight movement at the far end of the cellar caught her eye. She continued to move as though she were alone, releasing the safety on her gun as she walked.

'No need for the gun, Mal.'

She jumped, and let out a small scream at the sound of Derek's voice. 'What the hell?'

'Your little traps don't work on me, honey. I know how to breach your defences.'

Derek never ceased to surprise her. He'd left no trace of his entrance into her home.

She stepped toward him, tears springing into her eyes, her voice shaking. 'Trafford said you were dead.'

He stood up and winced. 'Well my love, the Cat had a red-hot go at finishing me. He stabbed me here.' He pointed to the left side of his ribs.

Mallory frowned. 'But how did you get away? How did *we* get out of there?'

Derek's eyes flicked sideways. He smiled and stepped toward her, enveloping her in his arms. 'I had to save you, babe. I managed to knock him out.'

She put her arms around Derek, glad he was alive, yet suspicious. She felt the pain seeping out of him. It seemed unlikely that he had managed to overpower the Cat with a knife in his ribs.

'Where's the Virgin Rainbow?' she asked.

He stepped back and looked at her, his blue eyes wide with concern. 'I thought you had it?'

'I woke up in a nunnery with no gun, no opal and no idea, Derek. Now I discover you're in Canada too, and in the cellar of my home on the day I return.'

He shook his head. 'A nunnery?' He looked as if he would burst out laughing. 'Look, can we continue this upstairs, Mal? The cold down here is really starting to make me hurt.'

Concern overrode her suspicions. 'How long have you been down here?'

'Three days. I wanted somewhere safe from Trafford. I was pretty sure he didn't know about your place. Even if he did, nobody would find this cellar.'

Suspicion and fear pricked at her again. The carpet over the cellar door was tacked down. She did a mental scan of the rooms upstairs. There was every possibility Derek had an accomplice up there somewhere.

He was already moving toward the stairs. 'Come on Mal, let's sit on the couch like we used to do. Maybe we could even go for a hike in the mountains, for old time's sake.' He grabbed at his ribs as he climbed the stairs. 'When I'm healed, of course.'

She shook her head. 'You can't stay here, Derek. We have to find the Virgin Rainbow, or Trafford will come after us.'

He stood at the top of the steps and looked down at her, his pleasant expression gone. For a moment, she thought he intended to drop the door on her, and trap her underground. Despite knowing that she had an escape tunnel at the far end of the cellar for just such an emergency, her heart lurched. It would take two days to wriggle up the tunnel to freedom. She jumped up the steps two at a time.

He smiled as she stepped into the bedroom. 'You always were in a hurry to chase after me, Mal.'

She decided it must have been claustrophobia making her imagine the worst of him.

They sat on the couch with hot coffees, watching the

afternoon turn to dusk in companionable silence.

He waved an arm at the view. 'I forgot how beautiful it is here, Mal.' He looked at her, his eyes dark with emotion. 'I forgot how beautiful you can be.' He reached toward her, and stroked her cheek.

She pulled back.

'What's wrong?' he asked. 'You always wanted to make love here…'

'Not anymore. Not with you.'

He curled his fingers around her neck, pulling her face toward his. 'For old time's sake, babe.'

She pushed against his chest, causing him to grunt with pain.

He dropped his hand, his expression hard. 'Are you saving yourself for your Australian copper, my love?' His lips twisted into a sneer. 'You really are a daft mare. He's Federal Filth. He would arrest you without thinking twice.'

'Why are you here?' she gasped.

'Finally, the girl asks a question worth answering.' He stared at her with contempt. 'I certainly didn't come here to hide, or win you back, you silly cow. I came here to tell you that I win and you lose... again. You'll never find the Rainbow.' He ran a hand through his hair, as if exasperated at having to explain. 'But Trafford, or the Cat – one of them, *will* find you. One of them will have their pound of flesh.'

'But they'll come after you too!'

'I'm dead and buried, remember. You're just a dead girl walking.'

The words from the note in her wallet rang through her head.

'Why would you put me in a nunnery?'

He laughed, gripping his ribs in pain as his deep baritone echoed in the silent house. 'I didn't, but dear God, what a masterstroke.'

He stood and walked to the front door. 'We saved you Mal, so that when the Cat gets out, he has a mouse to chase, and Trafford has someone to kill.'

'We? Who are you working with?' She went after him. 'I'll hunt you down, you bastard. I won't stop until I get the Virgin back.'

He saluted. 'Bye babe. It's been average.' He slammed the door and skipped lightly down the steps, his laughter floating into the mountain air, as if his wounded ribs were no longer an issue.

Out in the forest, inky shadows settled under the heavy stands of Spruce on the perimeter of the clearing. Derek's laughter, and the clear notes of his merry whistling, travelled across the quiet clearing and over the trees, slowly fading as he strode toward the road. Further away, the roar of a high-powered car reverberated through the valley, the sound swelling as it came closer. It stopped at the end of the long driveway. The driver revved the engine impatiently until Derek came into view. He stepped into the car as the night sky exploded into a blanket of new stars, and did not look back through the tinted windows when the car leapt into motion.

The man waiting and watching in the shadows smiled, and pushed silently through the trees. He heard a wild presence in the woods to the left of him, stilled while the creature stopped and sniffed the air. The country was foreign to the man, the habits of its wildlife unknown. He waited until the animal moved away before continuing into the clearing. He stopped again at the sound of breaking glass inside, before moving with feline grace toward the light pouring out of the French doors at the side of the house.

***

Inside the house, Mallory threw her coffee cup at the door, but her aim was erratic. The cup hit a mirror in the hall, and both smashed in a satisfying hail of glass and ceramic. Angry tears streamed down her face. She started to cry, her sobs coming in ugly, guttural heaves. She couldn't believe Derek had worked her over... again! This time was even worse than when he'd abandoned her in Cuba. She rubbed the tears out of her eyes, and tried to pinpoint his motive. She couldn't understand why he would fake his death for the Virgin Rainbow. It was collectible sure, but not worth any more than one and a half million. As she tried to join the dots, she glared at the reflection of the room in the window, and caught a furtive movement behind her.

She spun without warning, kicking out, had time to see a masked intruder duck as her boot whizzed past his chin. He lunged at her, but she stepped sideways and punched. He grunted, shaking his head against the impact. She dropped, rolled, and pulled a gun out of a sling under the couch before leaping to her feet, ready to train it on the stranger, but he was already pointing his weapon at her. The world slowed down as she held her hands in the air and waited for the shot.

'Drop it.' His voice was muffled through the balaclava, but it sounded familiar.

She leant forward and placed the gun on the couch.

'Move!' He motioned with his gun toward the hallway. She walked as slowly as possible while she tried to think of a way to overpower him. When they were close to the door, he stepped in and spun her toward the wall, grabbing her arms and forcing them behind her back. She felt something cold on her wrists and heard the snap of handcuffs locking. She pushed toward the door as if to escape him, before slamming back into him with all of her weight. The pair went down in a heap on the floor, and the roar of the gun discharging made her ears ring. *Shit! She'd forgotten about the gun.* She screwed her eyes shut, waiting for pain to hit her.

She rolled off the intruder and backed away, but he didn't follow. He moaned, and she noticed the keys to the handcuffs still in his hand. She crawled toward him, twisting around until she caught them in her fingers. He groaned and twitched. She worked on the keys, trying to keep panic from taking over. When the cuffs finally clicked open, sweat poured down her face, and she breathed hard. *Her home was worse than central station tonight!* She stepped over the intruder, intent on getting what she needed and getting out of the house, when he whispered, 'Mallory, don't leave me here to die.'

Her eyes widened. She couldn't understand how she had failed to recognise his voice. She pulled the balaclava off, and gasped at his pain ravaged face.

10

'I guess I shouldn't have crept up on you like that,' Sam said. 'But, there was no need to shoot me *there*!'

Mallory cradled his head in her arms. 'Stay still, I'm going to look at the wound,' she said.

The shot had entered his thigh close to the groin, and appeared to have missed the bone. She glanced at his face and realised he was waiting for her to speak.

'Don't worry, you'll live to be a father, as long as you stop creeping up on folk,' she said.

His expression relaxed, but his head dropped heavy onto the floor, his face pale.

Mallory glanced at the wound again. Her relief was short-lived when she saw the amount of blood soaking into the rug. She took off her t-shirt and wrapped it around the wound, before cupping his face in her hands. 'Don't you dare die!'

He touched her face, and slumped into unconsciousness. She flew to the phone, dialling with a shaking hand.

'Niall? It's Mal, I have to bring someone.' She stopped for a moment, listened intently. 'But he's lost blood, and he's in shock. He needs a doctor.' She stopped and listened again, before shaking her head. 'Come on little brother, you can't say no. This one's a lawman.'

***

Mallory stopped at a nondescript intersection half an hour later. She kept glancing over her shoulder at Sam. His eyes were closed, his face pale, his chest barely rising. She saw blood seeping through the blanket wrapped around him. She wouldn't think about him dying. She would get him to Edmonton. Niall was a magician when it came to gunshot wounds. *He would make it right.* She started to cross the intersection, and almost collided with a police car. She braked, smiling apologetically at the officer. He slowed, and stared hard at her as he cruised past, but he kept going. She let go of the breath she was holding.

When she reached her brother's house, she drove through the open gates and around to the back of the house. Niall opened a door, waiting with a stretcher while she backed the car as close as possible.

She jumped out, pulling open the back door while she spoke. 'Entry upper thigh near groin, exit just below buttock. The wound is clean and no bone damage, but he's lost a bucket of blood.'

Niall slid him out of the car onto the stretcher. 'Is this your handiwork?'

'Not exactly.'

'Christ, you can't keep expecting me to fix your shit. I could lose my licence.'

'Tell me off later,' she snapped.

They lifted the stretcher together, jogged through the door into his day surgery, and placed Sam on a bed.

Niall unwrapped the blanket, and went to work setting up a drip and cleaning the wound.

'How do you know this guy?' he asked.

'Long story. He's an Australian cop.'

'Is he in Canada hunting you, or is this your way of saying you don't want a second date?'

She sighed. 'Real funny. This was an accident, Niall. You know I'd never shoot anyone if I could avoid it.'

'Problem is, you can't avoid it in your line of work.'

'It's a sideline – you know why I keep my hand in.'

'Dad's gone Mally. You have to accept that he's probably dead.' He wrapped a clean bandage around Sam's leg and adjusted the drip, before looking up at her. 'Let it go. Hell, look what happened here tonight. You think this couldn't happen to you?' He frowned, 'And do you think this couldn't have happened to Dad a thousand times?'

She shook her head. 'Stop it. I know he's out there somewhere.' Her voice broke. 'He wouldn't abandon us. I know he wouldn't.'

Sam stirred and opened his eyes a fraction, but the siblings were too engrossed in conversation to notice.

'Come on Mally. Stick to the wildlife photography. Get out of this, before you disappear forever too.'

Mallory was shocked to see unshed tears gleaming in her brother's eyes. It had never occurred to her that he worried.

She jumped up and hugged him. 'I have unfinished business. Derek really put me in it this time.'

'What?' Her brother pushed her away. 'I can't believe you would go near that nasty lowlife again. It's as if you *want* to die young!'

Sam groaned, and the explanation Mallory intended was forgotten. She went to him and took his hand. He opened his eyes.

'Sam, it's okay, you're safe.' She smiled, but he didn't smile in return.

His eyes drifted to Niall. 'Thanks for saving me, mate.'

'What happens next?' Niall asked.

Sam looked at Mallory. 'You know I have to arrest you.'

She pulled her hand away. 'You're in no position to make threats.' She grabbed her keys, backing away from him.

'Where are you going?' Niall asked.

'I told you, I have unfinished business.'

'You're not leaving him here.'

'Why? You've done nothing wrong.'

Niall stood in front of the door. 'No. I won't let you do this to me, or my family.'

She stopped, defeated.

He put a gentle hand on her shoulder. 'There's a set of crutches in the storeroom. I'm going to have dinner with my wife and children, who by the way, have no idea you are here. When I come back, you will both be gone.' He glanced at Sam and lowered his voice. 'Maybe it's time to accept that we'll never find Dad. Maybe it's time to face the music and start over, Mally.'

After he closed the door Mallory paced up and down, jiggling her keys while she considered her limited options. There was nothing stopping her from leaving without Sam. She toyed with the idea for a moment, but who was she kidding? She would never go against Niall's wishes, or endanger his family.

Sam watched her. 'Do you want to tell me about your father?' he asked.

She shook her head.

He motioned to the chair beside his bed. 'Come on. We have time. I won't be good to travel for a few hours.'

She sat down, and played with the hem of the blanket. 'I didn't know it was you, but still, I didn't mean to hurt you. I didn't mean for the gun to discharge.'

Sam reached out and covered her hand with his. 'Yeah, I know. You're a bit crazy, but I reckon you could've found a less painful way to show you weren't interested.'

He smiled as he spoke, and Mallory felt the same connection she had on the day they met. A comfortable warmth coursed through her body and butterflies performed enjoyable flutterings in her stomach at his touch. She suddenly needed to tell him why she had to keep looking for her father.

'You know, Dad never stayed anywhere for long,' she said. We were always travelling, always chasing the next big thing. Life with him was fun and exciting – you never knew what was coming next. There were always crowds of people hanging out at our house. Everyone used to call him a modern-day Robin Hood.' Mallory shook her head, and smiled. 'I know he wasn't giving to the poor, but he was a good man, and a great father.' She paused. 'Anyway, one day he didn't come home. No one has seen or heard from him for ten years, but I know he would never abandon us. He's still alive. I won't stop looking for him.'

He stroked the inside of her palm with his thumb. 'Where do you think he might be?'

The sensation of his finger on her skin was distracting. She wanted to reach out and run her hand over his face. Instead, she withdrew her hand so he wouldn't feel the shiver running through her body. 'I have no idea where my father could be. I can't believe he would stay away from us, if he had the choice.'

'Why do you think he's still alive?' As soon as he asked the question, Sam wished he could take it back. Mallory looked like she had just been punched in the stomach.

'Why don't you sleep,' he said. 'I'll wake you when it's time to leave.'

She shook her head. 'No. I think we should go now.'

***

Mallory stopped at the gas station in Red Deer. She paid with cash, and studied Sam through the window while she filled the car. He looked too pale under the foggy glass and fluorescent lights. The clunk of the pump handle shutting off jerked him out of his sleep. He frowned in confusion at her.

She opened the door. 'Do you want to use the restroom? I can help you.'

He nodded and swung to face the door, groaning and swaying as he tried to stand. She put her arms around him, pushing him against the car for support. The air cut through their clothing, and a shudder ran through his body. She tightened her arms, leaning into him, unable to resist the urge to press her body against his.

He dropped his head onto her shoulder for a moment, before moving her away. 'I need the crutches.'

She looked up at him, trying to stop her mind from wandering to thoughts of kissing him. His gaze was glassy, and he seemed to stare through her. Panic curled inside her. What if he died here, far from the country he loved? There would be no way to return him to Australia without alerting the authorities and revealing her location. She stepped away from him, feeling the full force of the icy morning through her jacket as she grabbed the crutches out of the boot. He took them without comment and hobbled toward the restrooms. She watched him struggling with the door and felt sick. It was clear he was suffering, and she hated the fact that she was the cause.

When they were back on the road, he said, 'You have to give me the Virgin. If I take it back home, it will go better for you.'

Mallory shook her head. 'I don't have it, and I don't know where it is.'

She felt his eyes boring into her, and kept her own on the road. 'Derek double-crossed me. He was at my place gloating about it. I'm surprised you didn't see him.'

'Yes, I saw him. I thought you were splitting the bounty.' She heard his disbelief loud and clear.

'I woke up in a bloody nunnery with no idea how I got there. When I got home, Derek was waiting for me. He made sure that I knew he'd shafted me again. Right now, the guy who hired me will kill me, unless I bring him the opal, and Jimmy the Cat is after me as well.' She paused, swallowing the fear that threatened to engulf her. 'So, you are the least of my problems. I have to find Derek. I have to get that bloody opal back.'

Sam reacted to the fear in her voice. He put his hand on her arm. 'We'll find him together. We can worry about the rest of it later.' The warm steadiness of his hand calmed her. She glanced at him, and the warmth in his eyes lifted her heart.

The pair fell silent, each one seemingly caught in their own thoughts as the car passed through the silent, frozen countryside. Mallory remembered the mornings she'd spent with her father and brother, playing on Snow Racers, throwing snow balls at each other and running through heavy drifts to keep warm. When they came back to the house, her mother always had hot chocolate and marshmallows waiting. Life had seemed so simple then, as black and white as the snow-capped Rockies that surrounded their homes. She glanced at Sam. He dozed, his head rocking gently with the motion of the car. She slowed as she approached a roadside motel and gas station, and let two pickups pass. The vehicles sprayed dirty snow onto the windscreen, before disappearing nose to tail into the night. She shuddered. There would be no second chance if they lost control at that speed, on this road. She returned her attention to the vacancy sign blinking in the frosty air. It would be easy to leave him behind in a warm room, but how would she get him into the motel without waking him? She accelerated. Best to let sleeping lawmen lie.

**

Sam woke, and stared bleary-eyed at the parking lot. He shivered, rubbing at his arms to ward off the chilly air inside the car. He couldn't see Mallory. He sat up, groaning when his thigh grabbed, reminding him that he was wounded. He checked his watch and resigned himself to the obvious. She was probably long gone.

Mallory pulled the driver's door open, and handed him a steaming cup of coffee. 'You can't leave Canada without trying a large double-double from Timmies.' She jumped in and turned the key. Hot air blasted out of the vents.

'I thought you'd done a runner.'

She glanced at him over the rim of her cup. 'I wouldn't do that, Sam.' She pointed at the steam her breath created. 'I've been gone less than ten minutes. If I left you here in your condition, you'd die of exposure.'

'Where are we?'

'Near Calgary airport. I called in some favours while you were sleeping. Derek is on his way back to Australia.'

Sam frowned. 'Why would he do that?'

Mallory shook her head and stared out the windscreen. 'Don't ask me to second-guess that bastard's motives. All I know is, I'm going after him.'

Sam leant over and took her hand in his. He looked deep into her eyes.

His expression changed. 'I'm sorry, Mallory. I have to take you back with me.' He reached over with his free hand and locked handcuffs onto her wrists.

11

THE couple on the travelator looked like normal tourists after a long-haul flight. The dark glasses the man wore did not hide his exhaustion, and her clothes were crumpled and stained. As they neared the end of the travelator, he leant heavily on his companion and winced when he stepped onto solid ground. She smiled, flicking her silver-blonde bob out of her eyes as he put his arm around her shoulders. A dark-haired man ahead of them stopped and turned to scan the crowd. Before his gaze reached them, the couple busied themselves with removing layers of clothing that had been needed in the Canadian winter.

The man started walking again and the couple followed, careful not to get too close. They split at customs and went to queues either side of the man, before following him to the domestic terminal bus stop. The man studied them at the bus stop, smirking when she held her engagement ring up to the light, losing interest when they kissed.

When the bus arrived, the couple were the first on, and went to the very back. The man with black hair sat at the front and studied each new arrival. When the bus left the terminal, he pulled out a phone and held it to his ear.

At the back of the bus, Sam and Mallory exchanged glances. They knew Derek didn't suspect them, but they couldn't move closer now. Derek swivelled in his seat as he spoke, searching the faces of every commuter. Mallory wrapped her arms around Sam's neck and pulled him toward her, shielding her face from Derek's scrutiny.

Sam was so close to her, and the kisses they had just 'acted' were still fresh on her lips. She felt his breath on her neck and her skin tingled. It was impossible to maintain professional balance when he was that close. He looked into her eyes, and hot excitement fizzed between them. She snuggled into his chest and felt as though she were melting into him. The feeling was so delicious, she was close to forgetting all about Derek.

The bus slowed, and Sam pushed her away as he looked out the window at the entrance to the domestic terminal. It irked her that he could break the spell of their physical chemistry so easily, even though she knew he had no reason to trust her. She pushed the thought away and concentrated on tracking Derek. They waited until he entered the terminal before leaving the bus. It was easy to follow his path to the Qantas desk. Even in disguise, his natural flamboyance remained.

'He'll only travel first class, even on a domestic flight,' said Mallory.

They waited until he moved on to the members' lounge before approaching the desk and buying two economy tickets to Brisbane.

***

A sodden wall of heat hit the travellers as they exited the Brisbane terminal, causing the already tired commuters to wilt in the cloying, tropical summer. Mallory hitched at her t-shirt impatiently and wished she had time to change into shorts in Sydney. Up ahead, Derek looked as cool and collected as always. He lifted a nonchalant hand and waved a cab on. Sam was turned to one side, speaking in low tones into his phone. Mallory put a soft elbow into his side. 'He must be meeting someone here.'

Sam nodded and pocketed his phone. 'You can stay with me for now. I've cleared it with the boss.' He looked at the taxi queue.

'Shit. We need to hire a car or he'll get away on us.'

'Well, go hire one. I mean, you're on crutches. There's no way you can move quickly.'

He looked at her, as if measuring her flight potential.

She scowled. 'I've got more to lose than you, lawman. If his ride gets here before you get back, I'll get the number plate, and I'll get a good look at the driver.'

He hesitated. She knew he was considering cuffing her to him. She shook her head. 'You do that, you'll give the game away.'

Sam glanced toward Derek. He was staring at them intently. Sam dropped his head, so the cap he wore covered his face. He pulled Mallory close to him and said in loud, American drawl, 'Come on, honey, don't fret. I'll hire a car and get you out of this heat.' He wrapped his arms around her waist, pulled her close, and spoke in her ear. 'He's looking at us, Mal.' He lifted her chin and kissed her. Out of the corner of his eye, he saw Derek's attention slide away.

He rubbed a soft hand on Mallory's cheek. 'He's lost interest.' He let go of her and limped toward the rental car office in the terminal.

Mallory watched him for a moment. She could still feel his hand on her face, his lips on hers. She dragged her attention back to Derek. He was grinning broadly at a white Audi as it pulled into the curb beside him. Mallory lifted her bag, using it to push her way through a group of tourists. The Audi started to pull away from the curb.

A young woman grabbed her shoulder. 'Will you take our photo please, miss?'

Mallory shook her head and lurched through the group toward the road. She could just see Derek through the tinted glass, leaning toward the driver. Mallory squinted, but the car angled into the traffic, causing sunlight to reflect off the windscreen. She caught a flash of blonde hair and a feminine profile, and felt an unexpected stab of anger at the thought of him getting on with his life, after what he had done to her. She pushed her anger aside, focusing on the number plate instead, memorising the letters and numbers.

The car was long gone by the time Sam appeared in a rental sedan.

Mallory threw her bag in the back and jumped into the passenger seat. 'Ok, you need to get a fix on this number plate.' She watched him punch the numbers and realised she was holding her breath.

He looked up at her and frowned. 'The car is registered to Trafford Sykes.'

'That's impossible.'

He stared at her, his eyes hard. 'Is it?' His arm snaked out, quick as whip. Before she realised what was happening, the cuffs were locked on.

His phone pinged. She heard a person speaking on the other end. 'We got him, sir. Heading north on Gympie Road.'

Sam revved the car and accelerated into the traffic, ignoring the blowing of horns and screeching of brakes.

'Where are we going?' Mallory asked.

He kept his eyes on the road. 'You have the right to remain silent. Anything you say or do may be used against you in a court of law.'

Mallory swallowed hard, trying to push back the tears welling in her eyes. *Nothing made sense. Was it possible that Trafford, Derek and Jimmy the Cat were in this together?* No, she couldn't imagine Jimmy working with Derek, and she couldn't understand how Trafford would profit from the arrangement. *But the details didn't matter; she was dead either way*. Her head felt like it was caught in a vice, and she realised she was starting to hyperventilate. There was no point in fighting. She curled her body into a ball and stared out the window at the fluffy clouds drifting above the car. 'Sorry Niall, love you little brother,' she whispered.

Mallory woke, straining to make out shapes or sounds in the silent blackness. Was this what it felt like to be dead? She moved her arms, felt the cuffs bite into her wrists. No, the cuffs would be gone if she had passed over to the other side! She sat up and felt into the darkness with her hands, found the edge of the bed, and almost toppled over. The room seemed unnaturally dark. She wondered if she'd been drugged and thrown into solitary. She felt an internal scream of panic trying to escape, and heard her breath rasping in the darkness.

A sudden sound to the right of her made her stop breathing. A key turned in a lock, and she flopped onto her side. Light flooded into the room. The door closed, and she opened her eyes at the same time as a light switch was flicked.

'Good, you're awake,' said Sam.

She squinted up at him, relief coursing through her. 'Where are we?' she asked.

'In Far North Queensland. A place called Mackay. We've been on the road a long time.'

She sat up. 'Where's Derek?'

He looked around the room, his expression flat. 'I don't have to give you details.'

'Sam, for Christ's sake! Why would I give you the numberplate if it would incriminate me?'

He shrugged. 'Who knows what fun and games your type gets up to.'

'I need to go to the restroom.' Mallory held out her hands.

' When you're done, we're taking a run to the local station. They'll take care of you from here.'

'You bastard! You won't get near Derek. Look at the

state you're in. You can hardly walk! And he's too bloody smart for you.'

'Really? I got near you. None of you are as clever as you think you are.'

Panic, hurt and anger rose in Mallory. She lunged at him, wanting to hurt him the way he was hurting her. He grabbed her and easily held her away.

'I thought you were –' he stopped. 'I don't like being taken for a fool.'

'Neither do I! You said I could stay with you.'

'I didn't know you were working with Derek and Trafford then.'

Mallory shrugged him off and shut herself in the bathroom. She looked at the tiny window over the cistern. There was no point. If she made it out the window, she wouldn't get far with cuffs on. She heard Sam's voice and pressed her ear to the bathroom door.

'When did Jimmy escape?'

Mallory's pulse accelerated.

'I'm leaving her at the station. She'll be safer in custody if he's out.'

She rolled her eyes. *Bloody cops were all stupid to a man. Any fool knew there was no safety inside.*

***

The police station smelled of stale sweat and hopelessness, like every other station Mallory had ever had the misfortune to enter. She kept her eyes on the floor, answering each one of the processing Constable's questions with, 'No comment.'

When she stood up to go to the cells, he looked her up and down. 'Better mind your attitude in there.'

She resisted the urge to answer back. Lawmen were the same all over the world.

When the clang of metal gates locking down sounded, she let the last of her panic drain away. There was no point worrying about the worst that could happen. She was in it, and would have to find a way out. She sat on the hard bunk, folded her legs, and drifted into a meditative state while she turned the events of the past weeks over in her mind.

***

Sam waited for the Superintendent in a blank room at the back of the station. He opened the file on Warwick Cash. If he were still alive, he'd be in his late fifties now. Was it possible he had retired thirteen years ago, and relied on his daughter to make the money? Sam thought about the conversation he had overheard between Niall and Mallory. It was more likely the old boy was dead. Most likely at the hands of another criminal.

He closed the file and tapped the table with his pen. The Super should have been here by now. It was surprising how nervous he felt, but then he'd gone to Canada without permission, and brought a fugitive into the country without going through the proper channels.

A young man in a black suit stepped into the room, held the door open, and stared at the man following him with obsequious attentiveness.

The Super entered and glared at Sam. 'You look like shit, Walker.'

'Sustained a gunshot wound in the line of duty, sir.'

'Line of duty, my ass! You decided to go after a girl, and got your butt shot for your trouble.'

Sam's jaw clenched, causing a small tic near his ear. He held the Super's stare without flinching.

The man in the black suit stifled a chuckle.

The Super swung on him. 'Do you find it funny, Clementine?'

'No sir. Spot of indigestion, sir.'

'Right.' The Super turned back to Sam. 'I'm stuck with bloody Clementine because of you.'

Clementine reddened and stared at the wall behind Sam's head.

'As far as I'm concerned, you caused this shit show, Walker. You sort it out.'

'We're tracking Derek James, sir. We're trying to identify his companion. Mallory Cash is in custody.'

The Super flipped open a file. 'Well at least we managed to snare the invisible girl. Mallory Cash hasn't been seen in public as herself since she was thirteen, just before her father disappeared.' He pushed the file across the table. 'I'm sure it's not news to you, Walker, but all of these perps are believed to be the Cash girl. She's good, isn't she?'

Sam stared at the rows of photos. It was hard to recognise Mallory in any of them. He pushed the file away. 'I've told the guys to contact me if she decides to talk. We're on Jimmy Contanti's trail. He's heading north toward the Whitsundays. Derek James is heading that way, too. There's no sign that Trafford Sykes has entered Australia.'

'Stop boring me with the facts. Tell me something I don't know.'

'I believe the opal is still in Australia. Derek James will lead us to it, sir.'

The Super sat back. 'And the girl? Is she involved?'

Sam rubbed a hand across his forehead. 'She was in the beginning, for sure.'

The Super stood up, placing his hands, knuckles first, on the table. 'She may be a bloody chameleon, but I still can't believe she was right under your nose.' The Super straightened and folded his arms, his expression hard. 'And you didn't know.'

Sam stood and started to speak, but the Super held up a hand. 'You're the best we have in our division, Walker. You don't miss a trick, and yet you get up close and personal with an international jewel thief, the one you're supposed to be intercepting, no less.' He shook his head.

'And you had no idea?'

It was Sam's turn to redden.

The Super snorted. 'Come on, Walker. You're from the outback. You know how everyone knows everything out there. You know how they like to talk. Took intelligence five minutes to find out what was going on before the heist went down.' His eyes travelled to the wound area on Sam's thigh. 'Seems like she almost got you by the balls more than once.'

Sam went a deeper shade of red. 'I didn't know, sir.'

'I believe you... for now. Sort this mess out. Then we'll talk about the Cash girl.'

12

MALLORY sank deeper and deeper into her meditative state as she turned the events of the last month over in her mind. Now that she thought about it, Trafford's decision to employ her and Derek to steal the opal made no sense. His wife, Eve, was the best jewel thief in the business. He didn't need to hire outside help. Pieces of the puzzle started to click together. The 'sister' who had taken her to the nunnery; the blonde woman she'd seen in the Audi. Mallory's eyes snapped open. She didn't know why, but she was certain Derek was working with Eve Saldino. She jumped off the bunk, and yelled into the empty hall beyond the bars of the cell. The hall remained empty, so she grabbed the metal cup off the tray on her bunk, and clanged it against the bars as she yelled.

The officer who questioned her earlier burst through the door at the end of the hall and bellowed at her to shut up.

She stopped banging the cup. 'You have to get hold of Sam Walker. He needs to know that he's in serious danger.'

The officer smiled at her, but the sentiment didn't

reach his eyes. 'I tell you what, you tell me what the terrible danger might be. I'll pass it on to the detective.'

She studied his face. He was bluffing. She folded her arms. 'No. I'll only tell Sam.'

The officer rolled the keys over his fist while he looked her up and down. She shuddered inside, but stood her ground. He glared at her for a moment longer, before walking back through the door into the station. She collapsed onto the bunk and tried to contain the hope that was building in her. What if Sam didn't come? It was too terrible to contemplate.

She leaned against the wall and tried to work out why Trafford's wife would be in Australia with Derek. It made no sense. Mallory couldn't help grinning when she thought about the last time the pair had been in the same room. The tension in the room was so hot that day, it was amazing they didn't murder each other. There almost seemed to be sparks flying between them. Her grin faded. Yes, the vibe between the pair was almost electric. She slapped her forehead. *How could she have been so blind?*

Keys turning in the outer door broke her train of thought. Sam stepped through the door. A young man in a black suit followed and stopped just inside the door. Sam walked along the hall and stopped in front of her cell, his arms folded across his chest. He looked tired, stressed and short-tempered. Her heart thumped in her chest. She knew she'd only get one chance.

'I know how Trafford is connected to that car.'

He looked through her. She thought for a heart-stopping moment that he intended to leave her in the cell.

She stepped forward. 'Sam, please! You'll need my help.'

He shook his head, the movement so slight it was almost imperceptible. She glanced at the chubby-faced boy-man in the suit.

Sam slid the key into the lock. 'Tell the Super what you know. He'll decide what to do.'

She followed the men out of the cells into a small, stale-smelling booth. A door opened on the other side of the booth and a large man with a soft face and mild, brown eyes entered the room. He gave her a lazy smile and waved at a chair. 'Take a seat, sweetheart.'

Mallory felt panic rising. This man was dangerous; she would not be able to trick him.

He sat down opposite, clasped his hands together and continued to smile at her like an indulgent parent. 'You've landed in a spot of trouble. We can help you, but only if you help yourself.'

Mallory glanced sideways at Sam.

'Don't bother looking at him. He's in a similar spot of trouble.'

Sam's cheeks flushed.

Mallory looked the Super in the eye. 'He'll have more than trouble if you don't let me help him. Eve Saldino is in Australia. She's working with Derek.'

The Super leant forward, his eyes dancing as if she had just told him a charming anecdote. 'Now that is interesting. What do you think they're up to?'

She shrugged. 'I have no idea, but it's linked to the Virgin Rainbow.'

The Super nodded at Sam. 'And why do you think the best man I have on the force needs your help? You have something special to offer, perhaps?'

The young man in the suit sniggered.

The Super stared at him. 'Indigestion playing up again, Clementine?'

The young man grunted and stared at his shoes.

The Super raised a suggestive eyebrow at Mallory. 'Well? What special powers do you have that Walker can't do without?'

She felt the heat rising in her cheeks. 'I know how Eve and Derek operate. Interpol hasn't been able to get near either of them for years.' She leant forward, staring right into the Super's eyes. 'I'm sure you know how many operatives Eve has killed. Believe me, none of you will get close enough to get that opal back.' She sat back. 'Let's face it, I'm the best chance you have, and if it comes down to the wire, I'm expendable.'

The Super tapped his nails on the metal table. She felt her nerves jumping in time.

He stopped and thumped the table. 'Walker!'

'Yes sir?'

Mallory couldn't help admiring Sam's poise.

'I'm placing her in your care. She's a flight risk. Get a bracelet on her.'

***

Mallory stretched her legs and stared at the bracelet on her ankle. The electronic monitor was heavier than she'd expected. She glanced at Sam. His hands had been so gentle when he locked the bracelet in place at the station. His eyes flicked toward her and she smiled at the memory. The quick warmth in his answering smile made her heart lift.

As they travelled north, daylight was already departing and the long shadows of dusk claimed the landscape. Dark shapes rushed past the car, leaping and rearing into clumps of trees, or collapsing into deep, shrubby pockets along the roadside. Mallory stared at the alien landscape, and wondered how she would ever escape.

Sam slowed, stopping in front of a ramshackle hotel on the side of the road. A large statue of an Aboriginal woman clutching a baby overshadowed the front of the building.

'There's no point travelling tonight. Wait here while I find out if there's anywhere to stay,' Sam said.

After he was out of sight, Mallory stepped out of the car and approached the statue. A plaque at the bottom explained how a young Aboriginal woman had leapt to her death to avoid being killed by the police in 1867. Mallory looked at the scarred cliff face rising up behind the hotel and shivered. What if she were chased by enemies, and left to die in this foreign land? Niall would never know what happened to her. She would never know what happened to her father.

'The baby survived, you know.'

She jumped at the sound of Sam's voice. 'The baby?'

He pointed at the statue. 'Yes. She survived the massacre and was adopted by Europeans.' He waved toward the car. 'Come on, I've found an overnight cottage nearby. The hotel cook gave me some supplies. We'll rest tonight and arrive fresh in the morning.'

'Is that your entire plan?' she asked as she jumped into the car.

'No smartass, we'll work on that tonight.'

***

Mallory lay on the narrow bed and stared at the spreading mildew on the ceiling. Sweat rolled down her cheek, her eyes felt heavy from the heat. She thought about Sam's plan. It had flaws, but with the element of surprise and Sam's local knowledge, their chances were as good as they were likely to get.

He rapped on the door, and she frowned. He had a policeman's knock. She gave herself a mental slap. She'd noticed that knock the night he came to her hotel in Coober Pedy, and ignored it. It proved how dangerous a person's hormones could be.

'I've made dinner,' he said through the door.

'Ok.' She sat up, feeling heat-drunk and lightheaded for a moment. She dragged herself off the bed and stumbled into the tiny ensuite. She rinsed her face and stared into the mirror at the dark rings under her eyes, skin pale and shiny with sweat. There would be no point trying to use feminine wiles to get the better of Sam tonight. She dried her face, dragged a comb through her damp curls, and pulled on a clean t-shirt.

Mallory's cheeks burned when she entered the kitchen. The simple salad and bottle of wine on the table he had prepared reminded her of the night they spent together in Coober Pedy. He looked so good standing in the kitchen in a t-shirt and jeans, she wanted to rip his clothes off right there. She cursed her body, and hoped Sam would think it was the heat making her glow.

He leant against the bench, looking her up and down, before motioning to the deck outside the tiny kitchen. 'Let's eat outside.'

She ducked her head as the heat in her cheeks deepened, and grabbed her plate. His words were innocuous, but she felt certain she'd detected a spark in his eye.

After the meal, Sam poured more wine and threw his head back to stare at the stars blanketing the sky above. Mallory felt herself relax, as though her body were melting into the humid, tropical darkness surrounding the cottage. She knew Sam was relaxing too, and felt a moment of sheer happiness to be alone with him, despite the shrill whistle of crickets making conversation almost impossible.

He stopped examining the heavens and smiled at her. She realised she'd been staring at him. She poked her leg out. 'How about taking this thing off?'

His smile dropped, his face suddenly guarded.

'Come on,' she said. 'Where can I go here? And I couldn't outrun you anyway.'

He contemplated her through narrowed eyes. She rushed on before he could say no. 'Please. You can put it back on before I go to bed.'

He ran a hand through his hair and sighed. 'Ok.' He pulled a key out of his pocket and released the bracelet from her ankle.

He stayed beside her chair, looking up at her. She leant

down and rubbed her ankle. 'Thank you. It was starting to hurt.'

He reached out and touched her ankle with gentle fingers. She felt flames jump from her skin at his touch and withdrew her leg.

Sam jumped up, gathered the dishes on the table, and started toward the kitchen. Mallory collected the empty bottle and followed him inside. He dumped the plates on the sink and swung back toward the door as she placed the bottle on the bench. She collided with him and the touch of him made her pulse leap. She slid her arms around his waist without thinking, running her hands under his shirt along the smooth skin on his back. Her hands were on fire with the feel of him, and she moaned against his neck. She pressed closer to him, felt his breathing change, and looked up at his face. He looked into her eyes for a moment before taking her face in his hands and kissing her. His tongue found hers and she shuddered against him. He pulled her hips toward him as their kiss deepened. The heat rising in her body and the hammer of her heart against his chest became almost unbearable.

He stopped and put her at arm's length. 'You're so beautiful, but we can't do this.'

She pulled away without answering and walked toward the verandah, hoping to hide her frustration from him.

'Don't think about trying to run,' he said.

She turned back, her anger bubbling. 'Where exactly would I run? Let's just get this done. Then you can drop me at the nearest prison and get on with your life, lawman.'

112

13

MALLORY and Sam looked like any holidaying couple in love as they walked hand in hand along the Shute Harbour boardwalk. If anyone cared to look closely, however, they would see the tension in his shoulders, and the watchful expression on Mallory's face, as they scanned the yachts moored in the marina.

Sam nodded imperceptibly toward a vessel. 'There's the *Ellie May*.'

'What happens now?'

He smiled at Mallory. 'Follow my lead.'

When they reached the *Ellie May*, Sam called out 'Hey Robbie, where are you, old mate?'

A tall man, with a shock of white hair and deep tan, appeared from below deck. He smiled, revealing even, white teeth, as he climbed up the ladder.

He clapped a hand on Sam's back. 'How are you? Long time, no see,' before turning to Mallory and extending his hand. 'And you are?'

Mallory smiled and introduced herself. Robbie clasped

her hand in his, smiling warmly in return. It was impossible to guess his age, but she was amazed at the man's presence and wondered how many people he'd managed to disarm with his smile.

Robbie turned back to Sam. 'I've got some beers down below. Why don't we get underway, find somewhere peaceful? Have a drink and catch up, old mate?'

Sam nodded. 'Sounds perfect.'

After they were clear of the harbour, Robbie cut the motor and set the sails. Mallory smiled at a pod of dolphins jumping and splashing as they raced the yacht. She lay along the seat at the back of the yacht, staring at the endless sky above. She figured that surely, with all of the ocean and sky surrounding them, she was safe on this yacht for now. She smiled and really relaxed for the first time in weeks.

Sam stepped around the rigging and glanced back at Mallory's sleeping form. He turned to Robbie, 'Where are we headed?'

Robbie nodded. 'Hook Island. We can moor in Butterfly Bay. It's protected from the weather.'

Sam adjusted the mainsail. 'Do we have a fix on their position yet?'

'Yep. They're moored near Black Island.' Robbie looked toward the back of the yacht. 'Are you taking her with you?'

'Yes. I won't get close to them without her.'

The older man held Sam's eye, his meaning clear. 'You can trust her?'

'Yes. I believe I can.'

Robbie raised an eyebrow. 'Well, my friend, I won't argue with that. You'd better let her sleep.' He flicked open a map on his phone and showed it to Sam. 'I'll take you as close as I dare. I don't want to get too close. They may have better tech than we realise. You'll have to use the dinghy for the final leg.'

Sam frowned. 'What about back-up?'

Robbie handed him a tiny remote. 'Keep this with you. I'll moor where I drop you. If you need back-up, press that button. It'll set off a silent alarm on this yacht. Otherwise I'll stay put, and come when you radio the coast guard.'

The men stopped talking as they approached Hook Island. Both were intent on manoeuvring the yacht into the bay without using the motor. They moored a good distance from the shore and other yachts, before dropping the sails.

Robbie went below and reappeared with an esky. 'Let's have at those beers. Then you'd better get some sleep too. I'll wake you both in a couple of hours.' He nodded toward the shore. 'You may as well go for a swim, enjoy the serenity while you can.'

***

Sam touched Mallory's shoulder. 'Hey, wake up, you.'

Mallory came out of her deep sleep and stared blankly at Sam. The gentle sway of the yacht and clink of rigging further disoriented her, because she couldn't remember where she was. She sat up and looked around, her panic subsiding when she took in the beautiful bay surrounding the yacht.

She rubbed her eyes. 'Wow, I feel like I've been asleep for days!'

Sam smiled. 'Only a few hours.' He gestured toward the shore. 'Do you want to take a swim and have a look around the island?'

She frowned up at him. 'We didn't come here for a holiday.'

He laughed. 'Yeah, I know. We can't do anything until tonight, though. So why not enjoy the moment while we can?'

***

Robbie helped Sam and Mallory adjust their masks, before giving them a grin and thumbs up as they dropped into the water at the back of the yacht.

He pointed at the sun. 'Keep an eye out Sam-man. You need to be back here before dark.'

Sam returned the thumbs up and kicked away from the yacht. He followed Mallory's bubble trail, enjoying the feel of the warm waters across his skin. Tropical fish darted this way and that in front of his mask. He kicked forward and tapped on Mallory's shoulder, wanting to make sure she didn't miss the technicolour garden of corals beneath them. She turned and smiled when he pointed to the beauty below them. They took each other's hands and enjoyed the view below as they swam.

When they reached the shore, Mallory let go of Sam as they left the water, and walked onto the pristine beach.

He grabbed her by the waist. 'You are beautiful, Mallory Cash.'

She smiled. 'Thank you, Detective Inspector Walker.'

He winced. 'Ouch.'

She laughed. 'You're not bad for a cop.'

He cupped her chin in his hand and kissed her. 'Was that a compliment?' He ran his hands through her hair. 'God, you are so beautiful.'

The kiss seemed to take her by surprise, but then she pressed against him. When they finally stopped, they looked at each other, dazed.

Sam broke the spell. 'I want to show you the butterflies, and the spiders.'

Mallory's eyes widened. 'Spiders?'

He nodded. 'Yes. This island is known for the butterflies, but it is also home to an amazing number of St. Andrew's spiders.'

'St. Andrew's spiders?'

'Don't worry. They're harmless.'

He took her hand and led her into the mangroves beyond the beach. At every turn, colourful red and yellow spiders with huge cross-like webs filled the gaps between trees. They stopped at a web thick with spiderlings.

'There are so many,' Mallory said.

'Well, most of them won't survive,' Sam replied.

'Is that how you see it?' she asked.

He looked at her in confusion. 'The natural world doesn't make excuses. I don't pretend to understand everything, but I do understand nature. Do I think that everything in life is that cut and dried? Of course not.'

***

Mallory felt removed from him in that moment. It seemed their experiences were too different.

He put his arms around her and kissed her again. 'I don't pretend to know everything,' he said. 'But I know that I like kissing you.'

She leant into him then, giving her mouth to him, pressing her body into his. Their kiss seemed to go on forever, and yes, was over too quickly.

They continued hand in hand, enjoying each other's company in the silent interior of the island, taken in by the thick, coastal scrub covered in gossamer webs. Sam pointed out bird nests and signs of crocodile activity.

Mallory marvelled at the landscape, so different to the desert areas that Sam had shown her, and yet still so readable to him.

She stopped and picked up a shell. 'How did this get here?'

Sam laughed. 'I don't know. Not my country.' He looked at his watch. 'Christ, we have to get back to the yacht. Robbie, he'll worry.'

They retraced their steps, stopping for a moment to watch the sun dipping across the water, Mallory with a heightened awareness of the dangers they would face after nightfall.

***

Robbie grinned when he saw them at the back of the yacht. He gestured toward the smoking BBQ. 'We're in a National Park. No fish tonight, but I do have some of North Queensland's finest steaks cooking!'

He helped them onto the boat, stowing the snorkel gear while they dried themselves with towels.

When Sam slipped below deck to get dry clothes, Robbie turned to Mallory, his jovial expression gone. 'I'm sure you know that he's put his neck on the line for you.'

Mallory nodded, unsure how to approach the older man's protective hostility.

He folded his arms. 'You had better be on the level, or we will hunt you down.'

'We?' The question was out before she could stop it. His expression told her she should have stayed silent.

'Yes, the entire division. He's one of the best humans you could ever hope to meet. You play him, we won't stop till we find you.'

Sam reappeared from below.

Robbie smiled, his tone light-hearted. 'Hey old mate, I was just swapping fishing stories with Mallory.' He rolled his eyes. 'Fly fishing in Canada sounds like a total gas!' He gestured toward the fridge below. 'Grab yourself a beer. One won't hurt.'

Sam nodded and disappeared below.

He turned to her, his expression cold. 'No harm to him. Understand?'

Mallory felt a moment of sheer admiration. Robbie should not be underestimated.

***

The paddles sliced through the water without a splash as the dinghy moved soundlessly toward the yacht. Mallory scanned the darkness for the *Ellie May*, but it had already dissolved into inky night. She looked toward the bright lights of the yacht they were approaching, and tried to keep her anxiety at bay. All the same, she couldn't help admiring Sam's rowing style. It wasn't often that she witnessed a person who was able to move a dinghy through the water so smoothly. When they reached the bow of the vessel, he dropped the paddles into the dinghy without a sound, and grabbed a low-hanging fender, testing it with his weight. He lifted a thumb to Mallory and climbed the rope. He stopped for a second, looked up at the couple illuminated by the cabin lights on the deck above, and flipped over the safety wire without a sound. Mallory followed and dropped down beside him. She looked around and shivered in the humid, dusk air. They had no protection. If Derek and Eve turned around, there was nowhere to hide.

Sam grabbed his gun and signalled to Mallory to follow. She crawled along the deck behind him. She wished she had a weapon, because she felt certain she was going to die in this tropical paradise. It was clear to her now, that their plan was stupid. They reached the cabin and pressed against the lower wall.

She heard Derek murmur, 'Oh babe, I can't get enough of you.'

Her lips curled into a sneer and she almost laughed out loud. *The slippery bastard needed new material.*

Sam tapped her on the shoulder and nodded. She looked down at her naked ankles. She didn't owe him anything. She could get to the dinghy and make a run for it. The thought was fleeting. *She couldn't betray him, and besides, there was nowhere to go. She would die if she didn't help prove Derek and Eve were holding the Rainbow.* She rolled away from the wall and dropped over the side of the deck, hanging for a moment from the safety wire, before moving along the side of the yacht toward the voices.

She pulled herself back onto the deck, stood up and yelled, 'Derek!'

The couple in the cabin sprang apart, staring at her in shock.

Derek pulled out a gun. 'How the hell did you get here?'

Mallory raised her arms. 'Please don't shoot me. I've come here to help you.'

Eve stepped forward. 'We don't need your help.'

It took all of Mallory's control to keep her legs from shaking. Eve had no mercy. She knew the woman would kill her in a blink. She focused on Derek. 'Darling, you know I still love you.'

Derek smirked. 'What about the copper?'

'I didn't know he was a lawman.'

Eve threw her head back and laughed. 'She got tangled with the Filth?'

Derek shrugged impatiently. 'Who cares?' He cocked the hammer on his gun. 'What are you doing here, Mallory?'

'Jimmy Contanti and the law are on your trail. You'll need a distraction to get out of here.'

'Jimmy? Bullshit.'

Mallory saw the momentary doubt in his eyes.

'No bullshit. He's escaped.'

He shook his head. 'So? What's in it for you?'

'Tell Trafford I didn't take the Rainbow.'

Derek and Eve looked at each other and laughed.

Mallory saw Sam move into position. She dropped onto the deck and dived at Derek's legs, upending him before he could stop her. His gun discharged.

She crossed her fingers before jumping on his gun arm and biting his hand. He let go of the gun and howled.

Eve spun and aimed the gun at them.

'Stop!' Sam shouted.

She turned back slowly, looking him up and down, her eyes resting for a moment on his weapon.

'Mallory's copper,' she chuckled. 'Well, now I understand. Isn't he a pretty one?'

Mallory shuddered and levelled the gun in her hand at Derek. 'You hurt him and I'll shoot Derek.' She kept one eye on Eve. The woman had second sight, and a streak of evil a mile wide.

Derek uncoiled off the deck, smiling into Mallory's eyes. 'Oh Mallie, you couldn't shoot me.' He stepped toward her.

She let off a shot over his head. He dropped back beside Eve, his face pale.

'You are both under arrest for the theft of the Virgin Rainbow,' said Sam.

'You stupid, little man,' Eve purred.

Sam stepped toward the couple, and nodded at Mallory.

She kept her gun trained on Derek as she moved into the cabin, knelt down and opened the lockers under the seat. 'Fortunately, I know Derek very well. There's a good chance we'll find the Virgin on board.' She pulled out a leather bag and rifled through the contents, before holding up the opal in triumph.

The sound of clapping from the front of the boat made everyone freeze.

'Bravo, young Cash!' said Jimmy. 'Now play nice. I have something you want. I'm happy to give it to you for the opal.'

Mallory gripped the opal and shook her head.

Jimmy whistled. 'Really? You don't want to know where your old man is?'

The gun seemed heavy in Mallory's hand, and her feet felt like they were welded to the deck. She heard Sam telling her not to listen, but Jimmy's words were repeating in her head.

'Too late, time's up!' he shouted.

Mallory jumped and her arm jerked. Derek let out a howl and she realised she'd almost shot him. He glared at her, his face pale.

Jimmy laughed. 'Anyway Cash, you've saved me the

bother of torturing these two.' He ran his eyes up and down Eve as he moved closer to the group on the deck.

'Although it would have been fun.'

The woman's eyes narrowed and she hissed at him.

'Now, now, little Evie, why are you always trying to play with the big boys?' Jimmy raised an eyebrow. 'You and I both know what you're like, don't we babe? It seems to me that you owe Trafford big time.' He grinned and winked at her. 'I'm thinking your sugar-daddy's gonna be mighty pissed with you just now.'

She reddened and rushed toward him. He grabbed her by the arm. 'Now come on, that's no way to greet a man, after everything we've shared, *babe*.' He swung her around as he spoke, and punched her in the face.

Mallory was still trying to make sense of Jimmy and Eve, and didn't see Derek lunge toward her. He wrestled the gun out of her hand, and shot Jimmy before Mallory or Sam could react.

Jimmy staggered backwards and fell over the side of the boat.

Derek swung the gun toward Mallory. She dropped and rolled as the shot rang out.

'Drop it, Derek. My shot won't miss.' Sam said.

Mallory heard the gun hit the deck, and started to breathe again. She was moving to stand when a hand snaked around her throat. Eve lifted Mallory in front of her, using her body as a shield while she moved toward the back of the boat.

'Where are you going, Eve?' Derek asked.

If the situation hadn't been so awful, Mallory would have laughed at the hurt and disbelief in Derek's voice.

Eve heaved her into the dinghy tied to the back of the boat. She kept Mallory's throat in the iron grip of one arm while she pulled the cord on the outboard. When the motor coughed into life, she shoved her overboard.

'You were supposed to die in the desert, Cash, you dirty cop lover. I'll settle you later,' she called out as she gunned the engine and disappeared into the darkness.

The man in the desert, the 'First Lady' he talked about, suddenly made sense. Mallory couldn't work out why Eve wanted her dead, but now wasn't the time to consider the reasons. She felt the pull of the endless, black depths below her. There were sharks down there... and Jimmy. He was down there somewhere, too. She tried to control her panic as she swam toward the yacht, aware of the frightening possibilities contained in the inky water below. She surged toward the ladder on the back of the boat, but the waves seemed to be pushing her further away. She spluttered as she gulped salty water. She pushed through the waves with shaking arms until she reached the platform at the back of the yacht, dragging herself out of the water. When she could stand, she pulled herself up onto the deck in time to see Derek with his head in his hands while Sam read him his rights. He looked up when he heard her approach. She was shocked at the naked hate in his eyes.

'You fucking bitch! Shopping me to the law. I hope he was worth it because you're dead.'

Sam lifted him off the seat, spun him around with ease and cuffed him.

'After what you did, I was dead anyway,' Mallory said.

'Be quiet,' Sam said.

A soft splash sounded starboard. Sam took out another pair of cuffs, locked Derek to the rigging, and crept toward the sound. Mallory moved toward him, but he motioned to her to stop.

He waited, surveying the water at the side of the boat for some time, before returning to the cabin.

'What is it?' Mallory asked.

He frowned. 'Couldn't see anything, but that splash wasn't normal.' He went into the cabin and grabbed the radio.

Mallory leant back and let tiredness claim her while Sam talked to the Coast Guard. It was all over, but she was in more danger than before. She knew Trafford wouldn't let it go just because the opal had been returned to the museum. Once word got out that she'd shopped Eve and Derek to the law, she'd be just as dead as she was before.

Sam touched her shoulder. 'The Coast Guard is on their way. We'll wait for an escort back to shore.'

She stood up and looked into the black water surrounding the boat. 'Jimmy knew something about my father. He mentioned him when we were in the desert, too.'

Sam put an arm around her and pressed her head onto his shoulder. 'Don't get your hopes up. Jimmy the Cat is a lying bastard with nine lives, but I doubt he can survive a gunshot and the open ocean.'

Mallory pushed away from him and stared toward the coast. 'What happens to me?'

He glanced toward Derek. 'Both you and Derek will be under guard until this mess is sorted out. Then you'll stand trial. We have the Virgin Rainbow. That will go in your favour.'

'I'm dead, you know.' She shivered. 'It's only a matter of time.'

He pulled her into his arms. 'Don't worry. I do care what happens. I'll do everything I can to make sure you're safe.'

She pressed her face into his chest. 'I know you will.'

Derek snorted. 'Unless your "care" is bullet proof, old boy, she is a dead girl walking.'

Sam's arms tightened around Mallory. He glared at Derek over her shoulder. 'Shut up or I'll hang you over the side by your cuffs till the Coast Guard gets here.'

'That's police brutality,' Derek smirked at him.

Sam raised an eyebrow. 'What happens at sea, mate. I can't help it if you try to jump overboard and get hung up on your cuffs.'

A momentary leap of fear flashed in Derek's eyes, before he slumped against the mast in defeat.

14

MALLORY waited outside the door to the interview room. Even though the room was practically soundproof, she could still hear the muffled sound of the Super yelling at Sam. Clementine stood opposite her, staring at her chest as he rocked on the balls of his feet, his hands clasped behind his back like a nightclub bouncer. She glanced at him and he winked. She felt a slow, black tide of anger rising at the little prick's audacity. She stared at him, holding his gaze for a good minute before letting her eyes wander slowly toward his groin. She stared hard, then smirked. Clementine stopped rocking and covered his groin with his hands. Mallory looked up at his face, red now with embarrassment, and laughed out loud.

The door of the interview room flung open.

The Super glared at Clementine. 'What the hell are you doing hanging around here? Don't you have work to do?'

Clementine cleared his throat. 'I'm just guarding the prisoner, Guv.'

'Where's she gonna go in here? And don't call me Guv. You're not a bloody extra in *The Sweeney*!'

Clementine froze, his face brilliant red. Mallory felt a

moment of pity for him, and suppressed the urge to laugh.

The Super swung toward her. He jerked a thumb over his shoulder. 'You! In here now.'

She sat opposite Sam. He gave her a slight smile and kept rolling a pen around in his hand. She wanted to take his hands in hers, and hold them until his tension faded, but she knew the Super would make him suffer if she touched him.

The Super sat down beside Sam. 'You've got quite the record, young lady.'

She quelled the fear clutching at her chest and held his stare.

'We've got you bang to rights on a little 2013 job for a private collector in Paris. And then there's that little trinket you stole in Mumbai in 2015, and the job in Cuba with Derek James.'

'That wasn't me.'

He slammed the thick file he held onto the metal table. 'If you want our help, don't lie.'

'You can't help me.'

The Super took a manila folder out of the file and slid it across the table. 'Before you decide who can help, read this.' He stood and gathered the rest of the file into his arms. 'I'll leave it with you now, Walker.'

Mallory was already reading, and didn't hear the Super leave the room.

Sam watched her eyes widen, and cleared his throat.

She looked up at him with so many questions, she didn't know where to start.

He leant forward. 'It would be a new life, Mal.'

'No. It's consigning me to a life alone, in a foreign country.' She shook her head. 'What about Dad? What if he's looking for me?'

He reached out and placed his hand over hers. 'If your dad's out there, I'll hear about it.'

She sat back with her hands still caught in his.

He rubbed a thumb across her palm. 'Hey, I'll be

keeping an eye on you every step of the way. You'll be safe. Safer than you've ever been in your life.'

***

Sam lifted his nephew over his head as he sunk into the heat of the artesian spring, making the child squeal with delight. Flocks of colourful parrots burst out of trees higher up the gorge, their chatter adding to the cacophony caused by the child below.

Sam laughed and lowered him onto the rocks beside the spring. 'You're a noisy one, sunshine!' He reached out and tickled a toe. 'Come on Tau, you want to dip your toes?'

The boy's dark eyes danced as he dipped a toe in. 'Hot! Hot!' he laughed.

Sam moved closer and tickled his tummy. 'You're so dramatic. It's not that hot, mate.' He heard Mallory calling from the house, and winked at Tau. 'That's Miss Miriam calling you. Do you want to tell her where we are?'

The little boy jumped up and ran toward the house. Sam watched him for a moment before sinking back into the thermal waters. He knew it wouldn't be long before Tau returned with Mallory.

As he came up for air, he saw her standing with the boy, and smiled up at her. 'You coming in?'

She shook her head. 'Your sister is on her way. She wants to talk to you. Tau said we need to keep the perimeter safe.'

'I'm gonna get started,' the boy declared, as he released Mallory's hand and ran off.

He laughed as she slid into the water. 'I wonder where he gets these ideas?'

She shrugged. 'Don't know. He's a bit of a drama queen, like his uncle.'

Sam flicked water at her. 'Cheeky.'

Tau reappeared with a skink cradled in his hand, and

knelt beside the pool. 'Look what I found Uncy.'

Sam smiled. 'Put him on the rocks, son. Help him warm up.'

Tau lowered the lizard onto the rocks beside Sam.

The lizard froze for a moment before scurrying toward the nooks and crannies beneath the pool edge.

Mallory frowned at the departing lizard. 'He really shouldn't pick up reptiles without an adult with him.'

Sam squeezed her waist. 'Don't worry. He knows the difference between a skink and a snake.'

She hesitated, still feeling that she should say something to the child about the dangers lurking in the landscape, but he was already up and chasing after a large butterfly, his laughter bouncing off the steep walls of the ravine as he ran. She turned to Sam. 'How can you be sure he's safe.'

Sam stepped out of the spring and grabbed a towel. 'Nobody can keep him totally safe. All we can do is give him the skills he needs.'

She sighed and tried to avoid looking at Sam's chest and shoulders. 'I know you're right, but –'

He leant forward and brushed a soft hand against her cheek. 'Believe me, he's safer here than in most cities.'

Mallory felt a tap on her shoulder and turned to see Regina, Sam's sister, pointing at Tau. 'Look there, up there near the trees. He's spotted a big old sand goanna.'

'So it is. Don't often see them in here,' said Sam.

Mallory squinted and could just make out the shape of large monitor lizard sunning itself on the rocks.

Tau crowed in delight, hopping from one foot to the other. 'I knew it was a sand goanna, Mumma,' he yelled. 'I'm going to take a close look.'

'Only to the base of the rocks, Tau,' Sam called out.

The boy turned and looked at his uncle, his chin set in a stubborn line.

Sam raised an eyebrow at him. 'Give me your word.'

Tau nodded. 'Okay, only to the base.'

He took off toward the goanna, disappearing into the scrubby wattles at the edge of the clearing.

'Should we go after him?' asked Mallory.

Regina shook her head. 'No. He'll keep his word.'

She turned to her brother. 'Are you still going back to Sydney tomorrow?'

He nodded. 'I'll pull in and see Dad on the way back. I'll let him know that you'll be down there soon.' He pulled a t-shirt over his head.

'What about Miriam?' Regina asked. 'It doesn't seem right to leave her here alone, and she is Tau's nanny. I don't understand why she isn't coming to the Breakaways with me?'

Mallory frowned. 'I'm so sorry, Regina. I have relatives coming to see me here. I told Sam I would need some time out to see them. I should have told you as well.' She looked at Sam, her eyes flashing.

Sam folded his arms. 'My bad. What with the trip to Sydney, I forgot about your cousins coming.'

Mallory huffed. 'You're good at remembering stuff when it suits you.'

Regina rolled her eyes. 'I'm not hanging around to listen to another one of your stupid arguments. I'll go get Tau some lunch.' She walked toward the boy, who was still engrossed in his inspection of the goanna.

They watched her without speaking, the tension between them palpable.

Mallory broke the silence. 'I love looking after Tau. Why can't I go to the Breakaways with them? Not likely to run into anyone in the middle of nowhere, and I wouldn't get far out here if I tried to run. Why bring in the handlers?'

'What do you suggest? A night on the town in Melbourne? A quick jaunt to Perth for shopping as well?'

'Don't be a smartass! You must know how difficult this is for me?'

'I guess everything is about you?'

'Oh, great comeback! You're just angry because I won't –'

Sam sighed. 'Look, there's activity in Europe that has the Super concerned. That's why he's sending the handlers. Just ride this through, then we can talk about travelling with Tau.'

Mallory opened her mouth to protest when the sound of a helicopter in the distance made the pair pause.

'Long way off,' Sam said. 'Don't let it stop you from firing a new insult at me.'

She shook her head. 'No, listen. It's getting closer.'

The noise of the approaching aircraft started to reverberate off the walls of the gorge. Regina and Tau burst from the bushes and ran toward them. 'The old man goanna has run away,' Tau yelled. 'There's a big monster coming!'

Regina scooped the boy into her arms, her eyes locked on her brother. 'It's ok Tau, it's called a helicopter. It's just a machine.'

Sam scanned the sky. The whoomp of the blade rotations filled the air. Despite knowing it was coming, Sam jumped when the chopper suddenly appeared over the gorge. He turned to Mallory, about to yell at her to go with Regina and Tau to the house, but she was staring intently at the chopper. The look on her face stopped him.

She glanced at him. 'Jimmy!'

He stared up at the chopper, and saw the unmistakeable figure of Jimmy the Cat unfurling a ladder from the craft.

Sam turned and saw Regina and Tau reach the safety of the verandah. 'I need to get to the house. I'll shoot him.'

Mallory shook her head. 'What about the crew? You're not a stone-cold killer. Anyway, if he knows where I am, others will too. It's too late.'

She turned and looked at the house. 'No matter what happens, protect them first.'

Jimmy hit the ground with a soft thud and loped

toward them. 'Hiya lovebirds.' He glanced toward the house. 'I see you have company.'

Mallory stepped in front of Sam. 'What do you want?'

'Is that any way to greet a long lost pal, young Cash?' Jimmy asked.

'You're no friend of mine.'

Jimmy shrugged. 'Friend, enemy, family – all the same to me. I didn't come all this way to engage in semantics.' He thrust a folded newspaper toward her. 'Now don't refuse my gift, young Cash. I've gone through hell to bring you this. There's a photo of the Topaz Stallion on the front page.'

Mallory's eyes narrowed. 'So? Why bring me some old newspaper?'

'It's not old. Quite recent. Taken in Europe a month ago. A lone perp pulled off the impossible in Brussels. He had the Stallion on his left pinky.' Jimmy folded his hands and bared his teeth. 'Sound familiar?'

Mallory snatched the paper and flicked it open. She read quickly, before passing it to Sam.

She looked Jimmy in the eye and tried to forget how easily he killed people. 'So many people wanted that ring. It could have been taken from him. It could be anyone.'

Jimmy rubbed his jaw, his expression amused. 'They'd have to take off his dead hand.'

Mallory's face went pale.

He laughed. 'Yeah, I don't think that's what happened either. You see, he may have seemed benign to you, but not many people could kill your father. Even less could pull off that job in Europe. He always wore that ring on his left pinky. That heist has your father's mark all over it.'

'What would you know?'

His eyes darkened for a moment. 'More than you think, young Cash.'

'Why find me? Why tell me?'

He snatched the paper out of her hands. 'Well now, let's just say I've always had a vested interest in finding your daddy. I thought the more people looking –'

'I wouldn't help you, even if it meant finding my father.'

Jimmy shrugged, 'Suit yourself, young Cash. I'll find him either way. I found you, didn't I?'

He threw a hand up at the chopper and it started to descend. When it was close enough, he leapt onto the ladder, hanging in the air above her for what seemed like an eternity, before reaching into his vest. *This is it,* thought Mallory. *This is when he kills me.*

He pulled out the newspaper and threw it down to her. 'I don't need your help to find him. Of course, I prefer a challenger. I'm thinking a race for the Topaz Stallion would be more fun than just taking it off your father's dead hand.' He grinned and held up his hand like a gun at her, cocking his thumb as he spoke. 'Because that is what I intend to do, young Cash.'

The silence after the helicopter disappeared was deafening. Sam and Mallory stared at each other in shock, and might have stayed that way for hours if Regina hadn't called out to them from the house.

'What is the Topaz Stallion?' asked Sam.

'It's a ring. A very special ring that my father stole when he was a young man. The legend is that it's supposed to have protective powers.' She closed her eyes for a moment. 'I hope they have worked for Dad, because it is also coveted by every jewel thief and collector in the world. Dad vowed he would never part with it.' She opened her eyes, her expression worried. 'So, the fact that it has been seen recently means he's either dead and someone else has the ring, or he's alive and working again. I need to find out, one way or the other,' she said.

She grabbed Sam's wrist, unaware that she was digging her nails into his skin.

'You can't go anywhere,' he said.

She glanced toward the house. 'I'm going. You need to stay here, Sam. Keep your family safe.'

Sam shook his head. 'No. I won't let you go alone. You can't. And this place is compromised now. Regina and Tau will be safe at the Roadhouse with Annie, or the Breakaways with Dad.'

Mallory looked at him, her eyes fired with excitement. 'What if he's still alive, Sam?'

Sam drew her into his arms, hugging her close. 'There's only one way to find out.'

To be continued....

ABOUT THE AUTHOR

K. M. Steele is a dedicated word wrangler with a PhD in English Literature from Macquarie University. Her debut novel, *Return to Tamarlin*, was published in 2017, and she has articles, reviews, essays, poetry and short stories published in various journals, including:

Australian Book Review,
Australian ejournal of Theology,
Colloquy,
Transnational Literature,
and *Antipodes.*

Hawkeye Publishing signed her for her second novel, *Hunt for the Virgin Rainbow.*

To follow K M Steele, and hear about her upcoming
releases, including the second book in the
Hunt for the Virgin Rainbow series,
register for the newsletter at
www.hawkeyebooks.com.au
or follow her @KMSteele.author.

ACKNOWLEDGMENTS

Creative acts are not performed in a vacuum. They are always the result of the effort, support and feedback of many people. *Hunt for the Virgin Rainbow* is no exception. I thank my family and friends for always supporting me, even when I am at my procrastinating worst. Special thanks are due to Laurindah Taylor-Hambleton, Mark Kohler and Michelle Brock for reading early versions of the manuscript and offering insightful feedback; and Riley Stenhouse for his invaluable backstory brainstorming. I also extend my warmest thanks to Nicholas Birns, Candace Davis, Greg Reed and Cate Sawyer, who gave their valuable time to read *Hunt for the Virgin Rainbow* and write early reviews. Finally, thank you to Carolyn Martinez from Hawkeye Publishing for believing in my work, and making it shine.

A FAVOUR

Can I ask for your help?

I love writing fiction and I aim to entertain you. If you liked
what you read today, could I ask you to leave a positive review
or tell your friends about this book?

Book reviews can make or break a book.

Hunt for the Virgin Rainbow is available at
www.hawkeyebooks.com.au
and all good bookstores and libraries.

Find out what happens to Mallory Cash in the
Race for the Topaz Stallion,
available at <www.hawkeyebooks.com.au>
and all good bookstores and libraries.